THE LEGEND OF THE HILL

"The Hill will hold off as long as Riordan Truro's in it," Prowers said. He looked at Traylor with an expression that warned off possible levity. "Traylor, when Riordan says he talks to The Hill, what he means goes deeper than the understanding that comes from knowing rock, from listening to tommy-knockers and the shift of ground. He senses things, Traylor, that are easy to explain by saying they're damned good guesses. I've seen him stop and look at a roof that had been untimbered for years. He'd say...'Best be catching'er up!' More than half the time if we didn't...down she'd come!"

VOICES
IN THE HILL

STEVE FRAZEE

LEISURE BOOKS NEW YORK CITY

A LEISURE BOOK ®

January 2005

Published by special arrangement with Golden West Literary Agency.

Dorchester Publishing Co., Inc.
200 Madison Avenue
New York, NY 10016

ISBN 0-8439-5484-1

Visit us on the web at www.dorchesterpub.com.

VOICES
IN THE HILL

Table of Contents

Foreword

by
Eric Frazee

Steve Frazee was an expert on American history. All his stories were painstakingly researched for historical accuracy. The basic ingredients of a Frazee story include accurate historical descriptions, rich imagery, harsh reality, and the conflicts of the human soul.

Here are five of Steve Frazee's early works. They are reflections of childhood experiences gained from growing up in a Colorado mining camp in the early 1900s, his love of the history of the War Between the States, and his unique ability to explore the demons that live inside us all. . . .

Low Smoke

1

The vastness of the country below them was only something they could sense through the fog drifting in the trees. Every time they forced their weary horses a few yards on through the wet undergrowth, the gloom crept over where they had just been, and it was always there in front to strain their vision and make them wonder what lay beyond its edges.

Starr Purfield got down to lead his horse over a fallen tree. The blue roan stood trembling, blowing vapor that mingled quickly with the mist.

"Where are we?" Webb Hyslip asked.

"Somewhere across the Turrets. Even Coplon won't follow us this far." Purfield spoke softly, as if in deference to the unknown all around them.

"Any towns over there?" Hyslip asked.

"I don't know any more about the country than you do," Purfield said. He was a man of whip-thong strength and easy carriage. His eyes were deep blue with a sort of boyish wonder in them. He went on, leading his horse.

Hyslip swung down to put Guppy over the fallen tree. The sorrel sawed away from the obstruction, holding back. When it finally jumped, both hind hoofs caught, and it nearly fell. Hyslip was forced to one side, into wet bushes that soaked him with icy water in an instant.

Up ahead, Purfield began to curse as his horse threshed in a worse tangle. "It's a jackstraw mess of all the dead timber in the world! How'd we ever get into this?"

"Keep going," Hyslip said.

They had played one hand too many, that was all. They had tackled an express office in Arborville, Fred Coplon's own town. Coplon was a United States marshal whose presence in a territory gave courage to the citizens he protected. The express agent and a clerk did not turn into scared rabbits at the sight of pistols. Now maybe both of them were dead. Purfield and Hyslip had not got one cent from the deal. Anywhere ahead, or close behind them in the cursed mist, might be a slash-mouthed, silent man on a steeldust horse.

They came against a jumble of rocks and fallen trees, and there seemed to be no way out.

"If I ever see the plains again. . . ." Purfield shook his head. "Let's build a fire and let the horses rest."

"No fire," Hyslip said. "The smoke would drift along the ground for a mile. If Coplon. . . ."

"Damn Coplon!" Purfield said, but his eyes kept prying at the encircling fog. "It's supposed to be summer up here, and I'm half frozen."

"No fire, Starr."

When they were in the open and the sun was bright, it was Starr Purfield who gave the orders. It was Purfield who figured out how to pull a job to get quick money and not hurt anyone. But when they were all tired out and the future was bleak, Webb Hyslip took command.

They unsaddled. Hyslip took a shirt out of his bedroll and rubbed Guppy down. A fine, drizzling rain set in a few minutes later.

Purfield slumped down under a white spruce tree, rolled

up in his blanket. "We'll figure something out tomorrow."

Hyslip sat under another tree with his blanket around his shoulders. "Have you got any money at all? Or are you flat broke?"

"After that poker game in Chillcott?" Purfield said drowsily. "We'll get some more, don't worry."

They would get it, and then it would go like the rest. They owned the clothes on their bodies and two good horses with expensive gear. There were twenty-a-month riders who owned that much, Hyslip thought, and, when they had to spend a forlorn night like this, they knew, at least, where it was they would ride the next day. Hyslip wondered if he could ever be a hand again on someone's ranch. He doubted that Purfield could last two weeks taking orders.

In the cold wetness of the night Hyslip looked back on yesterdays without false regret. They had lived high on the hog. They had never hurt an honest man until three days ago. Perhaps if they had got away with the ten thousand supposed to have been handy in the express office, Hyslip would not now be remembering so vividly the two men they had shot. He was not sure about that, but for the first time in his life he was trying to come to terms with himself. Several times Hyslip stumbled up to quiet the horses when they tried to change their positions and grew frantic. Starr Purfield slept quietly.

In the morning there was a ghostly sun that did not cut all the way through the murk. The fog was still there.

Purfield wakened cheerfully, yawning, running his slender fingers through his thick black hair. "Things look better after a good night's sleep, Webb. Today we make our fortunes," he said, and laughed.

Hyslip began to saddle up. The blanket was damp, lathered yesterday, without a chance to dry last night.

11

"No breakfast?" Purfield asked.

"We got a fry pan with nothing to fry. We got a coffee pot with enough coffee for about two cups. We'll boil it when we're some place out of this mess."

Purfield laughed. "Suits me. A week from now we'll be rolling in the fat again, and we can laugh about this. You look sad this morning, Webb. Mosquitoes chew on you all night, or something?"

Hyslip put the damp saddle on Guppy. He did not cinch it. "I'm not rolling in fat any more, Starr. Not the way you mean it. I'm through."

"Oh, hell! We had a little hard luck and. . . ." Purfield looked around at the fog. "How could Coplon, or anyone else, ever find us in all this smoke?"

"I'm not worried about him," Hyslip said.

"I am . . . a little." The smile left Purfield's face. "Those two guys shouldn't have grabbed for guns, Webb. It wasn't their money. They didn't use their heads."

"That's a hell of a way to put it! That agent had a wife and kids."

"Uhn-huh." Purfield went to his horse. "Well, he should've thought about 'em. It was him or us."

"That's a damned poor answer, Starr!"

Purfield slapped the blanket on his roan so hard the animal tried to shy away. "The answer is . . . you've lost your guts. You've developed a streak."

Hyslip stepped over a log. He put his hand on his pistol. "What did you say?"

Surprise ran across Purfield's face. He stared at Hyslip for several moments. "That deal really did get under your hide, Webb." Purfield picked up his saddle. "All right, you're through. I'm not. Does that settle it?"

"It was settled with me last night."

Purfield grinned. "I shot my mouth off about you having a streak, Webb. You know I didn't mean it. We've said worse than that to each other."

The horses were rested, and they were hungry, eager as the men to get out of the forest. But the fog was always ahead and the tangles of fire-killed trees seemed endless. The drizzling rain was like infinity itself. Before long the stumbling over logs, the tearing of snags, the searing backlash of wet branches of the new growth timber drove the good humor from Purfield. "There's no end to this!" he said. "We should have tried to go around it when we first hit it."

They were in an old burn that might extend for miles. Hyslip said: "We can't do anything now but go ahead."

"That's wonderful advice. We should have. . . ."

Purfield shrugged his shoulders irritably. "Still got your mind made up?"

"Yes," Hyslip said.

"You'll look good, chousing old timber-running steers out of stuff like this for a living, holing up in some two-by-four line shack where the wind. . . ."

"Don't worry about that, Starr."

Purfield grunted. They fought on, and after a while Hyslip felt like shaking his fist toward a sky they could not see, and screaming curses at the fog. His clothes were torn by snags. They were soaked, holding the clamminess against his skin.

"Payment for our sins." Purfield laughed bitterly.

Sometime later Hyslip, in the lead, began to notice a change in the timber. The bodies of the trees scattered on the ground were lighter colored; the snags still standing were gray and ghostly in the fog. In normal weather the sun would be strong here. They were breaking out at last.

"We could ride now, if the horses wasn't all beat down." Purfield's tone was lighter.

Steve Frazee

The sun burst through, almost directly overhead. They were on a grassy hill with only a few dead trees standing high above the feathery growth of new timber. Behind them, high on the mountain, was the desolate burn they had crossed. Far on beyond the banks of fog they saw blue mountains that faded into each other.

Purfield laughed. "We're in a brand-new country, Webb! I'll bet Fred Coplon has never been this far from home." He began to hum. "How about coffee?"

"When we get to the edge of the trees below."

Hyslip hauled Guppy's head around as the sorrel snaked its neck for another bit of grass. He started downhill after Purfield. The grass was wet, and there was shale buried under the thin over-burden. Guppy's front hoofs slipped as the shoes cut down against the sloping rock. The sorrel did not fall, but came lunging ahead hard to hold his balance.

Hyslip felt the slackness of the reins and tried to leap aside, but he was still cold and tired and slow. Guppy's shoulder struck him. He staggered ahead sidewise against the only dead tree that lay within a hundred feet. With one hand he grabbed a long limb snag. It broke loose at the rotting trunk and let him pinwheel over the log into an outcrop of rocks below.

When he came to, there was smoke drifting across his face. Purfield's beard-stubbled face wavered in the air above him. "How are you, Webb?"

"All right." Hyslip's tongue was thick.

"Sure. Your ribs are busted, and for a while I thought your head was, too."

Hyslip could see the sun now. It had fallen far to the west in the time he had been lying here. He tried to rise, but he could not move. Purfield went to the fire and got the coffee pot.

"A drink of this will help." He tried to get Hyslip into a sitting position, but Hyslip's ribs were agony that flamed through his chest.

"Just leave me lay flat." After a time his headache dulled down, as long as he breathed carefully in shallow inhalations. "How many ribs?"

"Four or five, right under your arm."

Through half-closed eyes Hyslip stared at the sun. He was warm. He wanted to sleep. When the sun went down and he became chilled, he would get up and ride away on Guppy. "The sorrel . . . did he . . . ?"

"He's down in the grass eating his head off."

"Give me a few minutes to rest."

"Sure. Take it easy." Purfield grinned. "Still got your mind made up?"

Hyslip roused a little, and all the bitter facts came back to him. "I haven't changed my mind. I'm going east on this side of the Turrets."

Purfield nodded, and a moment later Hyslip slipped away into a half sleep. He came almost awake once when the smoke from the fire drifted low along the ground and made him cough and hurt his ribs. His vision increased gradually until he was looking past the fire and into the timber. Purfield was riding away on his blue roan, leading Guppy.

Hyslip tried to sit up and call out. The effort sent him rocking back against the ground with a groan. When he looked again, Purfield and the horses were gone.

The sun died soon afterward, and a cold wind ran up from the damp timber, brushing smoke across Hyslip's face. Well, he had intended to leave Purfield here, and Purfield had left him. Hyslip began to doze once more.

A trampling and the blowing of a horse aroused him. Someone came close to him in the dark, and then Starr

Purfield said: "How do you feel now?"

"You didn't leave?"

"Sure I did. I went after a deer."

Hyslip drank a few sips of coffee that night. He chewed weakly on deer liver. When he awoke in the morning, there was a shelter over him. He was covered with the stiffening deer hide.

Purfield was standing near the fire, shivering. "You sure made up for night before last, Webb. There's still a slug of java, boy. And deer steak."

"You're making that coffee stretch."

"Sure. The Swedish way. How do you feel?"

"Fine."

"That's a lie." Purfield grinned.

"You're lying about the coffee, too. You haven't touched a drop of it. I've watched you."

"Sure I have! I drank so much it kept me awake all night." Purfield got out the frying pan. He put lumps of deer fat into it and began to fry a steak.

11

They were ten days working down into the heart of the enormous flowing ridges and parks of the country between the Turrets and the far-flung western mountains that had no name.

Hyslip's ribs were still sore and touchy. For several days after his fall he had closed his eyes in pain every time he made a too brisk movement of his head.

They had talked no more of separating, but Hyslip's mind was unchanged. He had been too wobbly to tackle the ride along the east side of the Turrets, so he was going this way until they struck a natural parting place.

That was what he had told Purfield, but in the back of Hyslip's mind was the thought that they could go on together, after all. Webb Hyslip now owed the other man as much as he owed himself: they both should make a sharp, clean break with the past.

They rode to the edge of a mesa from which they looked for miles on range that had never been touched by anything but wild game.

Purfield couldn't trust the sight. "It's mighty funny there's no cows in here."

"You figuring on turning rancher?"

"If we had cattle, and someone to do the work. . . ."

Hyslip laughed.

"We hit a town," Purfield said. "We make a fast deal, and then we use the money to stock the best part of this with cattle. I. . . ."

"Not that way."

"How then?"

"I don't know," Hyslip said.

"It'll come easy, some way."

They rode from the mesa, Purfield humming. He was aroused and eager, with everything clear before him.

The seven riders took them by surprise that evening while they were frying deer meat.

Purfield drew his pistol.

"Put it away," Hyslip said. There were six rifles ready in the group coming at them.

It was the most magnificently mounted group Purfield had ever seen. Powerful horses, all claybank-colored, with the slender look of Thoroughbreds showing in the legs. In the lead was a red-faced man in the full uniform of a Confederate brigadier. Hyslip and Purfield watched uneasily as the leader lifted his mount across a little stream, scarcely bumping in the saddle. He rode up to the two men and raised his hand to signal those behind him to stop.

He was middle-aged, a heavy man whose uniform collar was buttoned snugly around a powerful neck. His eyes were wide-spaced and bulging. The other men were ordinary riders, Hyslip observed, but when they obeyed the bulge-eyed man in uniform, the whole effect was hard directness.

Guppy trotted to the end of his picket rope, whickering. The red-faced man turned to study the sorrel for a few moments, and then he looked back at the two men on the ground.

"How did you get into here?" The voice was startlingly high-pitched.

Hyslip pointed toward the Turrets' burned area.

"You came from up there, and you saw no one?"

Hyslip shook his head.

"Did you see the tracks of anyone?"

"No."

"When did you cross the mountains?"

"Three days ago," Purfield said.

The man studied them a moment longer. "The condition of your clothes would tend to indicate a longer period. If we startled you, I apologize," he said. "Allow me to introduce myself. I am Ambrose Sidney. These are my men."

Hyslip gave his right name. Purfield was so startled he did the same.

"With your permission, we'll camp here tonight," Sidney said.

"Help yourself, General," Purfield said. "We don't own a square foot."

"I know. I own it myself."

Hyslip blinked. "You mean . . ."—he glanced at the country rising in long ridges to the Turrets—"you own . . . ?"

"Everything," Sidney said. "The former Pacheco Grant. What is left of it, that is."

The Pacheco Grant! Hyslip had heard of it, one of the smaller Spanish grants, reputed to have been originally one million acres.

"You don't run cattle up this far, we've noticed," Hyslip said.

"I don't run cattle anywhere," Sidney said. "They are stupid creatures. I raise horses." He looked at Guppy out in the meadow. "By the way, sir, what is the background of that gelding?"

"Cow horse," Hyslip said. "A mustang chased Guppy's mother, and the rest is rawhide and wire."

"I have heard of the mustang strain," Sidney said, unperturbed. "And I've considered introducing it in my breeding . . . most carefully, of course. Wild blood has a way of cropping out to ruin the most handsome sort of product ten generations after its introduction. Someday I may put beef on this grass," Sidney went on. "I understand the Spaniards did, many years ago. But there's no hurry, sir, no hurry at all."

During supper, the odd details began to impress themselves on Hyslip. Sidney's men were all clean-shaved, or had been early that morning, at least. They did not talk a great deal, and what they did say seemed to be gauged for its probable effect on Sidney, who dominated everything even while silent.

The men were not Southerners, Hyslip observed. This was their second day out from the Vicuña Ranch, according to what they said, and yet they were nearly without food already. Late that afternoon, they ate most of the deer Purfield had shot, and then they lounged on the ground, smoking, talking but little.

After supper Hyslip gestured to Purfield with his eyes, and then walked casually toward the meadow as if to inspect the picketing of the horses. Purfield followed, grinning as soon as his back was to the camp.

"Ain't that general something?"

"Agreed. What's he doing out here?"

"Following two men that swiped a stallion." Purfield went over to his horse, checked the picket rope. "He was an infantry general in the war. He's one Southerner that didn't get ruined. He owns this country with a good title." He smiled. "He pays thirty-five bucks a month and needs men."

"You're thinking of going to work?"

"He's got three daughters, two young ones and one about twenty-two."

"Oh, I see."

"Well, we need work, don't we? For a while." Purfield grinned. Even with his ragged black beard he was good-looking.

"You know what happened the last time you tangled with somebody's daughter, Starr. I got shot in the shoulder taking a rifle away from her father."

"I haven't forgotten that, Webb. Look, you want a ranch. We both do, I mean. Maybe here's our chance to get it honestly. We work for the general and get in solid with him. We save our dough. He's got enough land here to give to a hundred people. Maybe in time. . . ."

"I know. I thought of it."

"Well?"

"Just don't get any wrong ideas about that daughter, Starr. The last thing I want is old Pop-Eyes on my neck."

Sidney assigned one-hour guard duty, including Hyslip

and Purfield. The general took off his uniform and hung it carefully on an aspen tree. From his saddlebags he took range clothing, donned it, and went to bed.

Sidney was up before dawn, shaved before breakfast. That, Hyslip thought, was in keeping with the man's character, but when his men began to heat water in frying pans and dig shaving gear from their saddle rolls, Hyslip and Purfield exchanged amused glances.

The first man to complete his shaving was a stooped, slight fellow with gray around the temples. There was a sort of blankness in his pale-gray eyes that gave a deceptive mildness to his expression. Hyslip had already marked him as a pistol man, the only one in the group.

Sidney said: "See that they are supplied with the necessities for shaving, Smallwood. They will ride with us."

Hyslip said: "Maybe we don't. . . ."

"It's best you go along," Sidney said. "It will afford me a chance to determine if I wish to hire you."

Purfield said: "Don't *we* have anything to say about that, General?"

"Of course!" Sidney's face was grave. "Give the razor to Mister Purfield, Smallwood, and then see that Mister Hyslip has one as soon as someone has finished. We will ride in fifteen minutes. Of course, you will have something to say about it, sir, subject to my view of the matter."

Purfield took the razor from Smallwood. "I guess we're working for the general, Webb."

Hyslip was the last one shaved and the last man up on his horse.

"If they didn't come this far, they've gone north on either the Florida or the Shavano," the general said, and Hyslip winced at the pronunciation of the names. "We'll find their trail today."

He was right. Shortly after noon Hyslip looked down at boot tracks in the sand beside Shavano Creek. "You mean they're on foot. I thought. . . ."

"We recovered the stallion and secured their horses, also, in an ill-considered night foray," Sidney said. "I sent the animals back to the ranch. Now I want the men."

Purfield and Hyslip looked at each other. As men who had lived outside the law they could not help feeling some sympathy for horse thieves.

The Shavano came down from the mountains through wide meadows. Along the fringes of the aspens the going was easy. Sidney spoke what was in Hyslip's mind.

"They should have gone into heavy timber, if they expected to get away. Somewhere there ahead in the rocks we should close on them today. Remember, they are not to be shot unless they force it upon themselves."

"Did these fellows work for you?" Purfield asked.

"They did," Sidney said. "Forward, gentlemen."

Within an hour the riders found the place where the fugitives had bedded down like deer in the aspen leaves, and then they had done just what they should not have tried—to beat mounted men to the heavy rock ridges ahead.

Late in the afternoon a shot came from the top of a low escarpment. The bullet went high above the posse. A voice called out: "That's far enough, Sidney! We'll drop those claybanks right and left if you try to take us."

Sidney rode out ahead. "Come down and surrender, Jacobs. You and Carswell will get a fair trial."

The man laughed harshly. "One of your trials, Sidney! How many claybanks do you want to lose?"

"Dismount. Bradbury and Arthur, take the horses to the rear," Sidney ordered.

Hyslip was glad to get down. An instant later two rifles

began to talk from the escarpment. One claybank went down with a grunt. Another screamed when a bullet struck it.

"Smallwood, flank their position from the right, with two men." The bulging eyes turned toward Hyslip. "Hyslip, you and Purfield go in from the left. Drive them off there or make them surrender. Don't kill them unless necessary."

Purfield moved first. "Come on, Webb. We'll make 'em think hell is five feet away!"

Hyslip followed him, running low through the trees. "He talks like a general, all right," Purfield said. "How'd we get into this?"

He was happy enough. He was always contented when there was action ahead, Hyslip thought sourly.

They took turns at pinning down the rifleman on their end of the hill. They alternated in making short rushes, using any depression or rock that offered the slightest protection. Smallwood and the other two were doing the same on the other side, the firing indicated.

Sidney walked into the open again. He signaled to the men left with him, and the fellows began to fire from the edge of the trees.

Those poor devils on the hill, Hyslip thought, *they should have seen they were boxed in. They shouldn't have shot the horses.* He had a brief, uneasy feeling about Sidney's promise.

Caught from three sides, with those who were coming in at the ends of the hill now so close that Jacobs and Carswell lost all the advantage of higher ground, the two horse thieves gave up.

They did not have the look of desperate men. Carswell was just a kid, sullen and scared. Jacobs was a tight-mouthed man, sweating and haggard.

"Where do they hold a trial in this country?" Purfield asked.

23

Smallwood nodded toward Sidney. "Him. He holds it."

When the two men were standing before him, Sidney said: "I promised you a fair trial if you came down without trouble. You ignored me, but you shall be treated fairly in spite of that. Do you recognize these two men, Smallwood?"

Smallwood hesitated. His eyes were unreadable. He nodded, and then he said: "Day Carswell and Jack Jacobs. They worked for you two weeks."

"Is that true?" Sidney asked.

"Why, hell, yes!" Jacobs said. "So we stole your stallion. You got it back, along with our horses. What else do you want?"

"You admit the theft, then. Carswell, were you unduly influenced or coerced by this older man?"

Carswell said: "I don't get what you mean, unless did he talk me into it. If that's what you mean, you ain't very smart. It was my idea."

Purfield laughed. He stopped when Sidney looked at him, but he kept grinning, nudging Hyslip. The surface of it was comedy, and Purfield was incapable of seeing deeper, or did not care to. Hyslip looked at the faces of men who knew Ambrose Sidney—and was afraid.

Sidney considered the two thieves. "You have admitted the theft of the stallion. Do either of you have anything to say in your own defense?"

"You got the damned stallion back, with interest!" Jacobs said stubbornly. "What else . . . ?"

"You, Carswell, do you have something to say?"

"Naw."

Sidney looked at his men. He smoothed the ends of his red sash absently with one hand. "The evidence is in. The men plead no extenuating circumstances." He pursed his lips. His face was calm, judicial. "Hang them."

Purfield was caught with a grin just forming. It hung

frozen on his lips. He tried to force it. He glanced at Hyslip, and then he stared in holy wonder at Sidney. "He doesn't mean it," he whispered.

"Carry out the judgment," Sidney said.

Matt Smallwood walked away. Sidney called his name sharply, but the stooped little man went on walking.

The others hanged the two men on a yellow pine tree. Purfield and Hyslip stood by and did nothing. Carswell went out cursing, his face pale and furious. They had to lift Jacobs into the saddle. Purfield did not see him go; he had staggered into the aspens, sick.

White splotches showed on Sidney's face. He stood like an iron man, and his will was like a physical grip on the men around him. After a while he said: "Bury them. We'll ride back to Vicuña in one hour." He turned about and walked into the aspens.

Smallwood came back then. "Boil some coffee," he said curtly to Everett Arthur. When two holes were gouged in the silt near the river, Smallwood spoke a funeral service.

They were drinking coffee when Sidney returned, wearing range clothing. He bundled his uniform carelessly into his saddlebags. He seemed to have shrunk, and the flesh of his face and neck had a flabby look. He glanced at Hyslip with an expression that was at once vague and appealing.

Purfield was no longer sick. He did not grin, but his eyes were bright when he said: "Working for him, there'll be something doing every minute."

111

Hyslip's first look at Vicuña was disappointing. The buildings sat at the head of a broad meadow dotted with horses.

There were enough corrals, and the barn was huge, of peeled pine logs, well-chinked, beautifully laid out, but the other structures were small and seemed to have been thrown together hastily, with bark still on the logs and the corners untrimmed.

He had been carrying in his mind the picture of a great establishment worthy of the empire it controlled. When the party went closer, Hyslip saw four men working on a stone foundation that was at least fifty-by-one-hundred feet in size. Two girls in bright dresses came from one of the buildings, yelling: "Daddy's home! Daddy's home!"

Sidney swung down and hugged them.

Two women came to the porch of one of the small buildings. They were of the same height, one a little heavier than the other, both black-haired. Hyslip stared at the younger one. She would be about twenty-one. Her eyebrows were dark, broad for a woman's. Her lips were full and red, with no expression of pettiness or sulkiness. Dusky was the word, Hyslip guessed, that he would use for her complexion. No, she was not at all like her father.

Purfield coughed gently, with the devil riding in his eyes. It was then that Hyslip saw Matt Smallwood, watching Purfield with a bleakly speculative expression. There was something about the little man that put a chill on Hyslip's thoughts.

They rode on toward a corral. Purfield was humming. Smallwood turned a little in the saddle to watch his face.

Purfield said: "Don't fret, Smallwood. I wouldn't steal a stallion, or even a filly." He laughed at the opaque, steady look Smallwood gave him. "You're the general's aide, aren't you?"

"I'm the foreman," Smallwood said.

After they had taken care of the horses, Purfield went with

26

a group toward what appeared to be a bunkhouse. It was mighty small for as many hands as Hyslip had seen. Apparently Sidney was raising horses first and letting details come along later

"Hyslip," Smallwood said as Hyslip started to follow the others when the last bar of the gate was up. "You and your friend didn't come over the Turrets when you said you did."

"No. It was a while before that."

"Does Fred Coplon want you two?"

"He might," Hyslip said.

"A killing?"

"We don't know. I'm going to find out as soon as I can."

Smallwood studied Hyslip for a long moment. "You've got something to think about, haven't you? Another thing . . . I'm willing to bet that friend of yours is not going to change."

"He'll settle down."

Smallwood looked deliberately to where Sidney and his oldest daughter were standing. Sidney's arm was around her shoulders. He was smiling. "If he doesn't settle down, he's picked the worst place in the world to be. Can you make him understand that, Hyslip?"

"I think so. But we're only working here, Smallwood. We're not your wards, you know."

Smallwood pointed east. "A town called Wartrace is building up fast over that way, just across the line of this grant. You know new towns. Sooner or later trouble will draw Coplon over there. I know him. He'll come up here as a matter of routine. When he does, Hyslip, I'll handle everything that comes of it. Understand that and see that Purfield understands it." Smallwood walked away.

He was, if Hyslip had ever seen one, a deadly little pistol man who would strike like a wasp. The picture of him speaking at the grave seemed far away now.

Hyslip watched Sidney go into the house. His daughter stood near the porch for a moment or two, and then she walked slowly toward a spring house on the hill. She moved with as much grace as Hyslip had ever seen in a woman. He wondered what her first name was. He wondered, too, if her moods changed like her father's. It had been a great many years since Webb Hyslip had escorted a decent woman anywhere. He began to roll a cigarette from borrowed tobacco.

He saw Ike Bradbury walking casually toward the spring house. Later, he and the girl were together, talking. It made a scene that could be read from a long distance. It did not last long. Sidney stepped out and called his daughter into the house.

Bradbury stood still a moment, then he started toward where the men were working on the foundation. A short, musical laugh stopped him. Purfield was standing at one corner of the bunkhouse, alone. Bradbury hesitated, then went on to the foundation.

Smallwood startled Hyslip by coming up behind him quietly. "We need men here, but we need trouble less. Are you sure you can handle your friend?"

Hyslip had a black moment of doubt about ever influencing his partner.

"Take care of him, Hyslip." And Smallwood walked away a second time, in short, savage strides, as if he would jar some torment from his system.

The days were not long enough for Ambrose Sidney. There was work to be done at Vicuña, and winter always came too soon. There was yet seven miles of fence to build to shut off a thousand acres at the lower end of the grant, to prevent horses from streaming back into the vast country toward the Turrets.

Sidney wanted the big house before winter, and an enlargement of the other living quarters. Out here on the fence line he was a good employer and a friendly man. Hyslip wished he had never seen Ambrose Sidney standing in judgment over two sullen thieves.

Purfield built fence with the rest. He was a better axe man than most men, but within a week his interest in the work was gone. He complained to Hyslip: "Old Bug-Eyes just wants to keep me out here all summer so I won't get acquainted with Kathleen. He's afraid of what a handsome young fellow like me might do."

"So am I," Hyslip said. "I don't need another rifle slug through the shoulder, Handsome."

"That Ike Bradbury . . . I bet he never smelled gunsmoke in his life. But he's there at the ranch, working on the house, walking out with Kathleen. . . ."

"He's gone," Hyslip said.

"Gone where?"

"How would I know? The cook told me yesterday. Bradbury's been gone for five days."

"Fired?" Purfield grinned. "Does old Bug-Eyes think that's going to keep ambitious lads away from Kathleen?"

"I didn't say he was fired, Starr. I do say that you're not the man to be setting your sights on her."

"Oh? I suppose you are then?"

"No. Nor any other hired hand, as far as Sidney is concerned. Forget it and behave yourself, Starr. We're reasonably safe here. We can hang onto our money. When some of the pressure is off Sidney, we'll get around to asking him if he ever intends to open up some of his land for cattle. There might be a chance to do here what we should have started six years ago."

"You got more advice than a minister. Do you and

Smallwood cook it up together when you're having those
little private talks at night?"

Sidney came out that day with ten men that looked to
Hyslip like barroom loafers and drifters. They were to finish
the fence, while the other crew went back to Vicuña to speed
up work on the house. He put in charge Everett Arthur, a
slow-moving, ponderous man who was really too big to do
heavy work himself.

Starr Purfield hummed and sang all the way back to
Vicuña.

Smallwood and Hyslip rode together. "You could have
left him out there," Hyslip said.

"No. Sidney's not satisfied with the corner notching on
the house, and he's watched Purfield swing an axe. Where'd
he learn that?"

"It comes natural to him," Hyslip said. Like a lot of things,
using a pistol, riding well, taking the main chance on a poker
game . . . and making himself attractive to women. "What
happened to Bradbury?"

"I sent him over the hill to find out why our sawmill was so
slow in coming. He'll be back."

"Then where will you send him?"

"Sidney had three sons killed in the war, Hyslip. Everything he felt for them is concentrated mainly on Kathleen
now. The governor of this territory wouldn't be good enough
for her. She's Sidney's daughter and I work for him, so I'll do
the best I can on both sides of the problem."

"I've seen girls handled like that until they got so desperate they ran off with any kind of saddle tramp," Hyslip
said.

The house was four logs high when Hyslip and the others

reached Vicuña. The next day it was down to the foundation stones again. Sidney had ordered the logs torn out. The corners did not fit to suit him.

"There will be generations growing up in this house," he said. "I want it built with that thought in mind."

Hyslip and Purfield did the corner notching, roughing down to the scribe lines with axes, finishing with heavy, curving gouges. The result was precise fitting.

The younger girls, Tony and Irene, were all over the job. They became at once attracted to Purfield because of his laughter and his stories about two bears named Blinkum and Stinkum. On the second day at the ranch, Mrs. Sidney sent Kathleen down to see if the girls were bothering the workers.

Kathleen asked Hyslip about it. "Not a bit," he said, "except I'm afraid they might get hit in the face with a chip."

If Purfield had seen prettier women than Kathleen, Hyslip had not. There was an expression of vigor and eagerness about her that made Hyslip forget for a while the six years of his own life just past. He stared at her until Purfield coughed gently.

Kathleen had not been unaware of Purfield, but now she looked fully at him. "You're Mister Purfield, the one the girls call Star Bright. They drive us frantic trying to retell your bear stories. You'll have to come up to the house some evening so we all can hear them."

Purfield grinned. "I bet your old man would love that."

Hyslip was startled. He expected to see Kathleen recoil from what he considered an ill-chosen remark. For a moment she looked steadily at Purfield, and then she smiled.

"He might have a bear story of his own, Mister Purfield . . . one about forward young men."

They were smiling at each other, and then suddenly they were laughing. Hyslip had seen it happen before when those boyish lights were running in Purfield's eyes. He was as handsome as they came.

"What do you think of this country, Miss Sidney?" Purfield asked.

"I like it."

"All the horses, too?"

"Every one of them. I've ridden since I was four."

"You must be good. Now, me, I need help getting into a saddle. I was wondering if some evening, saying your old man don't object, you could show me if these claybanks are good for anything."

"I'll consider that, Mister Purfield . . . saying my father doesn't object."

"If he does?"

"I'll consider that, too."

She and Purfield looked gravely at each other for a moment, and then Kathleen went away with the girls. Purfield began to hum.

Hyslip slashed his axe viciously into a log he was notching.

IV

Ambrose Sidney stood at the window of his living room, looking out at his daughter and Starr Purfield riding leisurely among the claybanks in his meadow. His eyes became more prominent, and then his neck began to darken.

"Merva! Merva! Why did you let her do that? The minute my back is turned, you women. . . ."

"Fiddlesticks," his wife said calmly, but her eyes were worried as she looked at her husband's rigid back. "He's an engaging young man, mannerly. I've no doubt he comes from a good family."

"I found him and Hyslip half starved and looking like savages! I won't have him and Kathleen. . . ."

"Riding out there on the meadow. You hold an intolerable tight rein on that girl, Ambrose, and there will be trouble. Forbid her seeing one man in particular and he will become immediately more attractive than all the rest."

Sidney glared from the window. He was afraid as well as angry. There was not yet a substantial man in the country, not one worthy of Kathleen. He recognized the truth of his wife's words, but he rebelled against acceptance of it. Suppose Kathleen lost her head over some worthless young vagabond? Sidney was no longer angry; he was only afraid. Losing Kathleen before the other girls were old enough to take her place would be like losing his sons all over again.

"When the time comes for me to pick Kathy a husband. . . ."

"For *her* to pick a husband," Mrs. Sidney corrected.

Ambrose Sidney nodded. He turned away from the window suddenly and sat down. "I ride myself, Merva. I wish I could leave it all in your hands and be satisfied. It doesn't matter whom she marries, as long as he's a good man. I had vision enough, even before the war, to know that our kind of life had worn out. I could see that the West would be a place where the qualities we thought we had in the South would weigh well. Everything is working out, but I still get all mixed up and disturbed about the war, and I keep remembering the boys. When I put on that uniform to do something I dislike, I suppose it's because I'm remembering Dick and Ronny and Jim, trying to punish myself . . . and others, too, because I didn't get out of the South when I first thought of it."

"That's all in the past now, Ambrose."

Sidney nodded. "I keep planning in the future, but so many ties go back to the past. . . ."

He raised his hand slowly to look out of the window. "Let her run around with her young men . . . a little. But let's don't rush things."

Both Hyslip and Smallwood were puzzled when no parental explosion came of Purfield's and Kathleen's companionship. They rode together every evening in the meadow, and sometimes the younger girls rode with them. Sidney ordered a jumping barrier built. Every time Tony and Irene put their claybanks over it, Hyslip winced.

Bradbury's return was delayed. He stayed away until he personally escorted the sawmill and the freighters across the east pass over the Turrets, then came on alone from Wartrace with the news.

Smallwood intercepted him when he arrived, and talked privately to him in the corral. Bradbury was hot and tired. Kathleen and Purfield were far down the meadow, almost out of sight, and Bradbury did not see them until he was going toward the bunkhouse.

The girl and Purfield came in laughing. Bradbury tried to be casual when he saw their faces, but all his hurt was on his own. Kathleen saw it. She was kind to him and tried to take interest in the details of his trip. That hurt him more, and Purfield made a monstrous insult of ignoring him altogether.

When Kathleen went to the house, Bradbury was still watching Purfield. "Let a man turn his back. . . ."

Purfield walked away to take care of the horses. There was no reason for his laugh.

"Go wash up," Smallwood said, and stepped casually in front of Bradbury when he moved toward Purfield.

"Now they'll hooraw him in the bunkhouse about getting cut out with Kathleen," Smallwood said to Hyslip after

Bradbury walked off in disgust. He spoke more loudly. "Sidney and I disfavor any kind of fighting trouble one hell of a lot, Purfield."

"Sure," Purfield said from a distance. "I'll remember that." He took care of the horses and went to the bunkhouse.

"That express agent and the clerk are all right," Smallwood said suddenly to Hyslip. "The agent is still in bed, though. His wife and kids are having a hard time."

"You *asked* Bradbury to find all that out?" inquired Hyslip.

"No. He was over there. It was news."

"Maybe he can put two and two together."

"He might," Smallwood said. "He's smart. If he does, he won't say anything except to me. He's a good man. I like Bradbury, Hyslip. I like him a thousand times better than your friend."

Smallwood went toward the bunkhouse in choppy strides, going, Hyslip knew, to keep his cold eyes on any trouble brewing between Purfield and Ike Bradbury.

There was no trouble immediately. It came later, after Kathleen and Purfield had been together at dusk near the new house. When they separated, Purfield went toward the bunkhouse, whistling. He saw Bradbury and laughed.

"I want to see you down by the corral, Purfield," Bradbury said, all his brooding rage threaded through his voice.

Smallwood was then in the house, talking to Sidney, but Hyslip had been prowling nervously outside, expecting this. He stepped from the shadows. "There's going to be no trouble, you two."

"Of course not," Purfield said. "Bradbury only wants to know how to keep a girl, in case he ever gets another one."

Bradbury cursed. He swung hard at Purfield, who moved

35

his head away as easily as a mule dodges a blow. Almost casually he knocked Bradbury sprawling into the lower rails of the corral.

"Stop it!" Hyslip said. He sprang at Purfield, and Purfield side-stepped, tripping him. Hyslip fell over the watering trough, and it seemed that he had broken his ribs again. He got up, gasping. Bradbury was charging back through the dusk. Purfield knocked him into the corral rails again.

"Like a wild bull," he said.

"Just stand still!" Bradbury shouted.

That brought them out of the bunkhouse and the main house. Sidney came running with Smallwood. When they got there, Purfield was backing away from Bradbury, with his hands out and open.

"Stay back, stay away," Purfield said. "I don't want any trouble, Bradbury."

Trying to fend off the other man's rush with his open hands, Purfield took blows in the face that rocked him back. "Lay off me, Bradbury!" He spun the enraged man, and only Hyslip could guess how neatly it was done.

Sidney said: "Have it stopped, Smallwood."

Bradbury slashed in again. Purfield stepped aside, and Bradbury smashed head-on into the corral logs. He clung there, dazed, until Smallwood leaped in to hold him.

"That's all, Brad," he said.

Purfield said: "I don't know what got into him."

"At six tomorrow morning bring them both to the porch of my house, Smallwood," Sidney said.

Hyslip's stomach tightened when he saw Ambrose Sidney standing in the early sunshine in his full uniform. Once more he was the martinet who had condemned Jacobs and Carswell to their deaths.

36

Bradbury and Purfield walked up before him. Purfield's expression was respectful, even a little awed.

"Your names?" Sidney asked.

He went through the preliminaries. It was travesty, Hyslip thought, but he knew also that it was not.

"Then there seems to be no reason for your fighting? Perhaps some of the others can enlighten me." Sidney asked the reason of the crew, calling names. One by one, men shook their heads.

Slim Dinkins said: "They just never did get along, Mister Sidney."

"That's odd, since they saw each other only briefly before Bradbury returned from his errand over the mountains."

Surely Sidney knew, Hyslip thought, he knew, but he refused to face the truth. He must make this legal mockery.

"Who struck the first blow?"

Bradbury looked at Purfield, who said nothing. "I did," Bradbury said.

"You were close, Hyslip," Sidney said. "Who struck the first blow?"

Hyslip hesitated. "Bradbury."

Sidney went on, gaining just the facts that were on the surface. They seemed to satisfy him. He said: "Vicuña protects all its members against outsiders. I expect loyalty and obedience in return. Fighting between members of my crew is a flaunting of my authority. Therefore, since Starr Purfield neither provoked this affair nor did more than try to stop it after it began, he is cleared. Ike Bradbury, the instigator, is discharged." Sidney's face was calm, judicial. "He will be horsewhipped and escorted to the nearest boundary line of Vicuña."

"No," Bradbury said. "No!"

"See to it, Smallwood," Sidney said.

There was a terrible struggle going on in Matt Smallwood. Hyslip did not give him a chance to make his decision. Hyslip stepped forward. "Mister Sidney . . . ?"

Purfield interrupted him. "Please don't do it, Mister Sidney." His face was boyish, pleading. "Bradbury is a good man. He lost his temper, that's all."

Sidney looked at Hyslip. "What were you about to say, Hyslip?"

Hyslip licked his lips. "About the same thing, I guess."

It hung for an instant. Then Sidney said: "The sentence is amended to discharge only. See that he's gone in ten minutes, Smallwood."

Later, when Hyslip and Purfield were notching logs, Bradbury rode away.

"What was it you were going to tell Sidney?" Purfield asked.

"The truth!"

"Didn't I tell the truth?"

"You were like a snake, Starr, about the whole thing. I didn't think it of you, either."

"In love and war. . . ." Purfield grinned. "Look, Webb, Bradbury and me were going to mix sooner or later."

"It was rotten, Starr. Let's have no more of it. I still don't see how Sidney swallowed that innocent stuff you gave him."

Purfield grinned. "He likes me. Like father, like daughter. Quit howling, Webb. I'm taking care of both of us."

"I'll take care of myself!"

Purfield raised his eyebrows. "Ain't we partners?"

You could not tell about him; you could not say how deep the boyishness went until it settled on deadly layers of his nature—or if, indeed, it was all pure mischief and no evil at all. Webb Hyslip chose to believe the last.

Everett Arthur rode in from the fence that morning. His face was bruised and cut, and he limped when he swung out of the saddle. But he was more bewildered than hurt. Sidney was supervising the selection of eight-inch logs for floor joists. He looked at Arthur coldly and asked: "What now?"

"I can tell you," Smallwood said. "He had some little argument with the fence crew, so he offered to take them all on at once to show who was boss."

Arthur's mouth opened and closed. "How'd you know?"

"Are they still out there?" Sidney asked.

"Sure." Arthur was miserable. "They like it as long as there's no work, and the grub holds out. They're playing cards and shooting at deer and. . . ."

"We'll change that." Sidney was at once arrogant and determined. He started toward the house.

"No good," Smallwood said. "There's ten men, and they're not going to stand still for you to hold a trial over them."

Sidney stopped. He stared at Arthur. "Good Lord! A man of your size and strength! You go back there, Arthur," Sidney said. "It's a reflection on me and Vicuña if you let them run you off."

"They already have," Smallwood said.

"Let me and Purfield go back with him for a few days," Hyslip said.

"Just let Purfield go," Smallwood said. "He likes a scrap. He can lick 'em with smooth talk and open hands." His hatred of Purfield ran viciously in his tone.

For the first time, it seemed to Hyslip, Sidney was sizing him up seriously. Sidney's eyes bugged out. His short jaw was shut tightly. He said: "Let's see what you can do, Hyslip. You take Arthur out there right away."

★ ★ ★ ★ ★

"How come you offered to take on the whole crew at once?" Hyslip asked Arthur on the ride out.

"I thought I could lick them."

For the first time in weeks Hyslip laughed.

They found the fence crew trying to barbecue a deer over a pit.

Somebody said: "Pee Wee run for help, and it looks like they was short of it at the home place. Where's the old lobster that wears a Reb uniform to hold court?"

The fence crew laughed; they were having a time for themselves. But some of them laughed too loud, glancing at the quiet smile on Hyslip's face.

"The general told you fellows that every man who works for him shaves every morning," Hyslip said, having dismounted. "It looks like some of you have slipped. You, Gruber, you'd better set the example."

"Well now, High-Slope, it'll take about six good men to convince me of that."

"He's here, all six of him."

Arthur grinned. "Two at a time?" he asked. "I can do that, all right."

"One at a time, until you get warmed up."

"I never got one good lick at you before, Arthur." Gruber flexed his shoulders and smirked.

Hyslip watched critically. As a fight, it was all power and enthusiasm. Gruber and Arthur hit each other often enough and hard enough to cripple an ordinary man. The enthusiasm never died in Gruber, but the power began to wane. Arthur slammed him into one tree after another, and then he picked him up and flung him toward the creek.

"I'm warmed up now," the foreman said. "Jones, you and Axford are next."

A man started to draw his pistol. Then he saw Hyslip, watching with a cold smile, and shoved it back.

Jones and Axford were game. They circled around Arthur like wolves around an elk. They pounded him and kept trying, but after a while Arthur gathered them both in and slammed their faces together. Both men sagged.

Arthur dragged them toward the creek. "When you come to, shave!" he yelled. "Michaels and Pomeroy next!"

Pomeroy was a squat, grizzled man. He shook his head. "To hell with you. You like to fight too well. Where do you want the fence built next?"

"That's it, I guess," Hyslip said.

"No, it ain't." Gruber was coming back from the creek. "You worked this thing out, High-Slope. Let's see if you can fight like you can figure."

Hyslip put his pistol on the stump.

He was amazed at the vitality of the huge, loose-lipped man. Gruber had been helpless a few minutes before, but now he was strong again, ready to go. Hyslip could not stand two of his blows, and he knew it. He ducked under swings that made Gruber grunt. He took one on the forearm and was almost thrown off his feet. He spun Gruber and hit him in the side of the neck going away.

Hyslip let Gruber wind wide and far, and then took him in the belly coming in. The gasp said it was paying territory, but Hyslip took a chance. He twisted low and surged up with an uppercut that carried all his power and weight from the spring of his knees to his shoulder.

Gruber caved in.

"Any other customers . . . one at a time?" Hyslip said. "I'm not Arthur."

"No, you ain't," Pomeroy said. "Arthur didn't knock him wedge-cold like that." He picked up an axe and started away.

41

"I'm going to build me a piece of fence. It's plumb interesting work."

"Stick around," Hyslip said. "We'll tie into that deer . . . after everybody shaves."

Before Hyslip left, he asked: "Now is everybody satisfied that Arthur's the boss?"

"Uh-yep!" Gruber said. Deer fat was dripping from his clean-shaven chin. He whacked Arthur on the back. "Him and me will have some high old times, drinking and scrapping of a Saturday night!"

When Hyslip returned to Vicuña, Sidney asked: "How many are left out there now?"

"Ten."

Sidney stared thoughtfully at Hyslip. "Can Arthur handle them this time?"

Hyslip nodded.

"I'll be damned," Sidney murmured, and said no more about it.

Purfield walked over to Hyslip. He smiled briefly, but there was an odd tightness around his eyes when he said: "What are you trying to do, Webb, work in solid with old Bug-Eyes?"

"Why not?" Hyslip could not say exactly why he had volunteered to go out and restore Arthur to his job, but he knew that he had enjoyed the task.

Purfield said: "Now, if you try to take Kathleen away from me, you'll really be getting somewhere, won't you?"

"I don't like the tone of that, Starr."

Purfield laughed. "Old Gloomy Gus!" He gave Hyslip a shove on the shoulder. "After all the years I've prophesied, you still get your fur up now and then."

"I can't always tell about you, Starr."

Purfield opened his eyes wide. "Me? Why, I'm a simple

boy from the hills. Folks read me like a book."

Smallwood came over from the blacksmith shop with a broad-bladed chisel on a long handle. "How'd you straighten it out?" he asked Hyslip.

"I suggested to Arthur that he take on half of them at one lick, instead of the whole gang. So he did."

"How about that Bill Gruber . . . how'd he take it?"

"He took a double dose."

"I thought he would. If he sticks around, he'll be a foreman here someday when Sidney starts opening up a little with cattle."

"I didn't know Sidney intended to."

"He does . . . someday."

V

The blast of sound from the Golden Bucket in Wartrace was a shock that reminded Hyslip that he had been a long time away from towns. He and Purfield stood on the walk before the place, with a month's pay in their pockets.

Purfield's eyes were bright and calculating as he peered through the window. "Faro, Mexican monte, poker. That poker game has a green look about it."

"You're wearing borrowed clothes, Starr."

"Don't remind me of that trip across the Turrets. I'm going to let these kind people in here buy us both new outfits. Don't come in right away, Webb. When you do, see how it's stacking up, and then we'll work the old crossfire on those green and verdant people."

"We were going to save our money."

"This is an investment. A man don't buy cows with thirty-five a month."

Hyslip bought himself a new outfit, a pair of gloves, tobacco. He went to a barber shop for a bath. Afterward, in the
Timber Palace, he had two drinks. And then he didn't know
what to do. Between the time he had made his decision on the
Turrets and now, something had gone out of him. The noise
of town had lost its old shine.

His eye was still sharp for men who might know him, and
in the back of his mind was the thought of Fred Coplon. A
man thought he was changing his way of life—and maybe he
meant it strongly—but there were things out of the past that
could not change rapidly.

He went out and stood on the street. Timber, cattle, and
mining. The marks of all three were on the town. It was a hell-
roarer, growing fast.

Hyslip went back to the Golden Bucket. Purfield's work-
tough hands, his beaten clothes, and his innocent face made
him look like a sheep among wolves in the poker game.

"You look like a man with wages in his pockets," Purfield said
to Hyslip. "Set in. I need somebody in my class that I can beat."

He was about even, Hyslip estimated.

There was a puzzled look on the gambler's face two hours
later when Starr Purfield, talking like a happy child, was
about twelve hundred dollars ahead. "You're the luckiest hay
hand I ever saw," the houseman said.

He concentrated on Purfield and, consequently, lost a
four-hundred-dollar pot to Hyslip a few minutes later.

"I got enough," Hyslip said, much to Purfield's disgust. At
the bar, Purfield said: "We could have cleaned up."

"Not when they threw another houseman in. We got
enough for one night. And I'll keep the money this time."

"All right, grandpa," Purfield said. "Just give me a hundred for a few little things." He grinned.

★ ★ ★ ★ ★

The next time Hyslip saw Purfield they were in Madam Beasley's place. Purfield was showing off a silver-trimmed bridle he had bought for Kathleen.

Before Hyslip and Purfield parted again, the latter drew another hundred dollars. Later, Hyslip met Everett Arthur in a restaurant. Arthur was worried. "There's some talk that Bradbury is looking for Purfield," he said.

Hyslip and Arthur found Purfield with Bull Gruber in the Cattlemen's Saloon. Ike Bradbury was at the end of the same bar. Hyslip crowded in between Purfield and Gruber, who was drunk. They had a drink together. A mocking light in Purfield's eyes told Hyslip that he knew exactly why Hyslip was here. It would not be a fist fight this time, Hyslip knew.

"Let's wander up to the show at the Golden Bucket," Hyslip suggested.

Purfield grinned. His glance went sidewise toward Bradbury. "That's a real delicate approach, Webb. Let *him* go see the show. I don't run away. . . ."

"He's no hand with a pistol," Hyslip said.

Gruber's voice was a roar. "He ain't afraid of Bradbury! He done licked him once!"

"Shut up, you fool," Hyslip muttered, but he knew it was too late.

Bradbury had heard. He had to make a move. He stepped out from the bar.

"I hear you're looking for me, Purfield," he said.

"I heard it the other way around, Brad."

There was Bradbury's out. Hyslip prayed for him to take it, but he knew how Bradbury's mind was working. The man had brooded for weeks.

Hyslip said: "Bradbury, there's no need. . . ."

"You can't throw me off, Hyslip. Shut up."

Hyslip felt that he could count the split seconds of clumsiness while Purfield let Bradbury start his draw. And then Purfield used his skill and speed deliberately. He shot Bradbury in the shoulder point. Bradbury dropped his pistol, reeling back. Purfield shot him in the corner of the mouth so that the bullet gored through the cheek, smashing teeth and ripping hideously.

Hyslip did not go over to look at the wounded man. Gruber did. He was oddly quiet afterward and not as drunk as he had been. "That shoulder is crippled," he said. He took a drink quickly. "His face is all torn to hell, Hyslip." He wrinkled his fleshy brow. "He started it. He forced it, didn't he? What was it all about anyway, Hyslip?"

Gruber was an honest man, probably no more dense than many in the room who had seen only what they had seen—which was that Starr Purfield had been forced to defend himself after giving Bradbury a chance to step away.

Hyslip and Purfield went to their room.

Purfield sat down on the bed. "What could I do, Webb? He was after me."

"You intended the whole thing, just like you tricked him there at the ranch. You crippled him so he could go through life remembering himself and Kathleen like it used to be. Why did you do it, Starr?"

"I guess I couldn't forget that he hit me." Purfield's eyes were bloodshot. He looked tormented, but in spite of that the youthful appearance of his face was untouched. "I'm sorry about it now."

"Sorry! You could have shot three inches left and never crippled his shoulder! He dropped his gun. You didn't have to shoot the second time at all."

Purfield stared at the floor. His dark hair was tousled. He

shook his head. "It was a hell of a thing. What will Kathleen say?"

There was no chair in the room. Hyslip sat on the floor and tugged at his boots. If he could get a few hours' sleep, his mind might not be so disturbed.

"How much have we got left from tonight?" Purfield asked.

"Around fourteen hundred. Why?"

"Why don't we send all of it over the hill to that express agent and the clerk? You said their families were having a tough time."

"You mean that?"

"Sure, I do. I'd sort of like to try to pay off a little for some of the things we did."

Hyslip was no longer angry. "All right. But what if it brings Coplon prowling in a hurry?"

"Put it in a package. Give it to Arthur and have him send a kid with it to the express office. Coplon might come over, but maybe the agent and the clerk won't even mention it. If Coplon does come, how far can he trace back on who sent it?"

Purfield undressed and got in bed. He was asleep at once.

Hyslip lay sleeplessly a long time in the dark. . . .

They sent the package the next day. Arthur did not know what was in it and asked no questions.

On the way back to Vicuña, Purfield hummed, admiring the silver-mounted bridle tied to his saddle horn. When they reached the ranch, Hyslip took care of both horses while Purfield went across the yard. Hyslip watched him give the gift to Kathleen on the porch.

The words did not carry, but Hyslip knew when Purfield was telling her about Bradbury. He saw her startled attitude, and he observed Purfield's lowered head and air of penitence.

Later, the silver-mounted bridle sent little sparkles of evening sun when Kathleen and Purfield were riding in the meadow with Tony and Irene.

Matt Smallwood found Hyslip at the corral. "The boys gave it to me as they saw it, Webb, but it reads some different to me. I told you before that I think a lot of Bradbury."

"What do you want me to tell you, Matt?"

"I just might have to cut down on your friend someday. Will I have to figure on you, too, then . . . or afterward?"

"Maybe Starr alone will be enough for you."

"That ain't much of an answer, Webb."

After Smallwood walked away, Hyslip kept looking down at the meadow, where Kathleen rode with Starr. Webb Hyslip was in love with Kathleen, and now he admitted it. It really went back to the first moment he had seen her. He wished it were a problem that could be handled as easily as settling a happy-go-lucky rebellion of the fence gang. . . .

After a long, hard day, Ambrose Sidney sat by the window. The cedar shakes were on the roof of the new house fifty feet away from him. Before long the inside would be completed. Furniture was on its way across the mountains now. Material things would always be around for the using. The country would not change radically if intelligence was used in the management of it. It was the human beings who must be selected, for people were always far more important than the land.

He nodded to his wife. "I've decided to send young Purfield out to the sawmill and keep him there to run it. He knew more about setting it up than the men who were supposed to be experts."

"And that, you think, will keep him away from Kathleen!"

"I didn't say that." Sidney blinked. "But that's exactly the idea. I've decided that Hyslip is the man for her."

"Is he?"

"Yes. I know men, Merva. Hyslip has every quality this country needs. He's steady. He's tough. He's. . . ."

"What does Kathleen think of him?"

"Why, how should I know? In time. . . ."

"You're not breeding claybanks now, Ambrose."

"Merva, sometimes you talk rougher than a stable-hand!"

"Admit what I said is true."

"I won't admit it!" Sidney said. "All I want to do is see that Kathleen gets the best husband possible, and I know who that is. That's all it amounts to. Webb Hyslip is the best man Kathleen could pick."

"You don't know anything about him."

"I'm checking his background now. He comes from a good family, as far as I know. He has four brothers, all successful cattlemen."

Merva Sidney sighed. "Personally, I like Starr Purfield much better."

Sidney frowned. "He has more natural mechanical skill than any man I've ever seen. If we'd had a few thousand like him on our side during the war. . . ." He shook his head, lost for a moment in something he wanted to forget. "But there's something lacking in that boy, Merva. He's dangerous."

"Fiddlesticks! He's charming."

"Not to me," Sidney said. "He's useful, but I can see through that surface charm into something I don't like. What he did to young Bradbury. . . ."

"He tried not to kill him, that was all. He told Kathleen so. He did everything he could to avoid unpleasantness."

"Maybe." Sidney stared perplexedly at his wife. He trusted her judgment, but he thought perhaps she was now influenced by remembering a former life in which charm and elegance weighed heavily. No, he decided, she was more level-headed than that. She simply was mistaken about young Purfield.

"I've got to go out to that lousy sawmill," Purfield complained to Hyslip. "I told you old Bug-Eyes would figure out some way to keep me away from Kate." He grinned. "Not that it's going to work."

"You set it up for him, didn't you, when the rest were fumbling around?"

"Sure! But a fool could run it now."

"That's why he sent you out there."

"I . . . hey! You haven't made a joke in a long time, Webb." Purfield gave Hyslip a shove. "You know, I'd sort of like to get out of here. We've been here a long time, getting nowhere."

"What about Kathleen? I don't want to see a fine girl take a bad fall, Starr."

"It never struck you that way before."

"Now it does."

A tightness formed around Purfield's eyes, but a moment later he laughed. "Stop worrying. I'll let you be best man when Kate and me get married in that nice new house. And then you can notch the logs for the one we'll have to have. And we'll be sure to name the first boy Webster."

Purfield rode away toward the sawmill, singing.

Two days later Sidney said to Hyslip: "Kathleen and the girls want to go buy some women's things in town. Drive the spring wagon, Webb. Keep an eye on them. You know what Wartrace is. Check the freight office for my furniture, and see if you can pick up five more men. You be the judge of them. I know I can trust you." He whirled away quickly.

On the way to Wartrace, Kathleen wanted to talk of

nothing but Starr Purfield. "You must have known him a long time, Webb."

"Yeah."

"I'll bet he was a demon with the girls."

"No."

"Were you?"

"No." Hyslip grinned when Tony and Irene giggled. Kathleen was laughing. The laughter loosened up something in Hyslip. He was able to talk more freely thereafter. It was a most pleasant trip to Wartrace, and he did not wonder at all why Sidney had sent him instead of Smallwood or the cook, as was usual.

Kathleen and the girls stayed at the Mansion House. Hyslip got himself a room above the Wartrace Saloon.

He took care of Sidney's business, and inquired about Ike Bradbury. The man was up and around, with a useless shoulder. Back in his room, Hyslip lay on the bed, thinking that if he could find any honest way to take Kathleen away from Purfield, he would do so. If there was any way. . . . But she was in love with Starr.

The next morning Hyslip waited three hours while Kathleen was having dresses fitted in a shop. It was afternoon before they started back to the ranch. Kathleen was radiant, satisfied with the trip, and sure she had forgotten half the things she had come to buy.

"What kind of gowns does Starr like?" she asked.

It occurred to Hyslip that the spangled cheapness of dance-hall girls' attire had always suited him fine. He said: "Most any kind, I guess."

"How about you?"

"I just like any pretty dress, I suppose," Hyslip said.

"Regardless of what's inside it?"

"I wouldn't say that." Hyslip smiled.

"You're a funny sort to be an old friend of Starr's, Webb. You're mostly serious, something like Matt Smallwood."

"As old and tough as all that?"

Kathleen smiled. "No, just sort of calm and thoughtful."

Hyslip studied her face. She was watching the crowds. The eagerness and strength about her was like the sun on the morning of a day when a man expected to get a good many important deeds done. She should always be strong and happy like that, Hyslip thought. But if she married Purfield, how long would it last?

An instant later his nerves set hard inside him. Fred Coplon, the United States marshal, was standing in the doorway of a livery stable. Tall and grim he was, a stringy man in ordinary clothing. No badge. No outward authority about him, except a feeling that came from his cold blue eyes. He looked squarely at Hyslip, weighing him. He let the wagon pass.

Hyslip drove to Vicuña with all his worries acquired from the present now subject to the past. He went at once to Smallwood. The little foreman turned bleak and gray.

"He knew you?"

"I'm sure of it," Hyslip said.

"He'll cat-and-mouse. He'll find out plenty before he makes a move." Smallwood was deeply disturbed. "Remember, I'll handle it."

"How can you? It's our trouble, not yours."

"Never mind. I'll handle it."

VI

The next time Sidney sent Hyslip to Wartrace, Kathleen went alone with him to see about her gown. Hyslip left her at the

Mansion House. He checked his pistol there with the desk clerk, and made every joint in town, looking for Fred Coplon.

There was no use to let the thing drag out forever, and there was an outside chance that Coplon, who was known for tempering his commission with personal judgment, might not have come to Vicuña because he considered settlement satisfactory in the affair at the express office. Hyslip had to know, one way or the other, but Coplon was not in Wartrace that night.

At midnight Hyslip went back to the Mansion House to reclaim his pistol. He was half a block away when he saw Starr Purfield go into the hotel. The lobby was empty when Hyslip got there. The clerk, not the one who had received Hyslip's pistol, was looking over his spectacles at a newspaper.

"Ah, yes," the clerk said. "One Forty-Four caliber for Mister Hyslip." He put the pistol and holster on the desk. "We have no rooms, sir," he said when Hyslip hesitated.

"What room is Mister Purfield in?"

"We have no Mister Purfield here."

"He just came in before me," Hyslip said.

"Oh! You mean Mister Stanfield. Room Two-Oh-Two."

The writing said Stanfield, but it was in Purfield's hand. Sick and angry, Hyslip went up to Room 202. There was no one there. He knew that was how it would be. He sat in a chair until four o'clock. . . .

Kathleen was happier than he had ever seen her on the drive back to Vicuña. Hyslip did the best he could to hide his thoughts and control his face. He waited until evening before he saddled Guppy and rode to the sawmill.

Purfield saw him coming and met him near the slab pile.

"The clerk told me this morning," Purfield said. "Don't be so damned sore, Webb. We're going to get married."

"When?" Hyslip snapped curtly.

"As soon as her mother and her get old Bug-Eyes softened up a little. Otherwise, we'll go ahead, anyway."

"Don't call him that name any more!"

"All right. You *are* damned good and sore, ain't you, Webb? If I had lost out to you, then. . . ."

"Don't put it that way, Starr."

"Why not? You've been in love with her right along. Who can blame you? By the same token, who can blame me for what happened?"

"I can. Fred Coplon might ride in any time and take us both away. What about her then? You should have thought of that, Starr."

"He won't take me away, Webb."

They stared at each other.

"If he doesn't, we'll be on the run again. The thing for you and me to do is go see Coplon now," Hyslip said.

"Give up? You're crazy."

"We're not going to shoot Coplon!"

"Of course not." Purfield spread his hands and frowned. "You're worrying too far ahead. Things will work out. We tried to pay off for some of the damage. What more do they want?"

And that was almost what Jacobs and Carswell had asked before they were hanged.

Hyslip rode back to Vicuña, knowing that he had accomplished little, if anything. He wondered if he ever would, in matters where Purfield was concerned.

Ambrose Sidney was taking more interest in Hyslip every day, coming around to talk to him, asking advice, giving Hyslip more supervision of the ranch affairs. The house was finished, and the Sidneys moved into it without fanfare.

Work began at once on enlarging the other buildings.

"We'll ride out tomorrow," Sidney said. "I want to look over some of the grant again, under more pleasant circumstances than the last time."

Going toward the Turrets the next day, Hyslip was impressed once more by the vastness and excellence of the range for cattle. He mentioned the fact.

They stopped on a mesa overlooking forage for ten thousand cattle. "One ranch, or split it up?" Sidney asked.

Hyslip's heart jumped. He answered slowly. "I'd make one ranch of the whole thing, with camps spread all over. I'd see that this range was taken care of."

"That's my idea, too. I've always considered cattle stupid creatures, but there's money in them. It's my plan, when I get my horse raising developed the way I want it, to go into cattle. It will take the right kind of men, Hyslip, men to look generations ahead. There's a future here. You bear that in mind all the time you're overseeing the piddling work we have to do to get ready."

They were going back to Vicuña when Sidney said casually: "You've got some rough spots in your past, haven't you, son?"

"That's right."

"You regret that?"

"The time for regret is before, not after."

Sidney eyed him keenly. A little later he said: "How do you and Kathleen get on?"

"All right."

"I know she's infatuated by your friend, Webb," Sidney said. "I consider that a temporary attachment. A young woman sometimes fails to see the qualities in a man, unless, of course, he finds some way to demonstrate them."

Sidney was pompous and there was a brutal streak of dominance in him, Hyslip thought, but blended with those qualities was a fumbling humanness that offset the rest. . . .

Establishment of regular mail service to Wartrace gave Kathleen an excuse to go every afternoon to town. Her sisters soon lost interest in the ride. It was not a long trip, but Kathleen frequently found reasons in advance for staying overnight. Sidney insisted that Hyslip go with her. After delivering her to the Mansion House, Hyslip never saw her again until it was time to call for her in the morning.

Just once he checked the livery stables late at night and saw Purfield's sorrel. He did not check again, but he knew the horse was there every time Kathleen stayed in Wartrace.

Then one night she sent a messenger to Hyslip, asking for him to come at once.

"He's in town, Webb, but he isn't here."

Hyslip set his face. "Who?"

"Don't act like that. You've known all the time." She faced him, standing. "It's over, isn't it? Did it last any longer than usual?"

Hyslip said: "Don't talk like that!"

She had not been crying. She was not explosively angry or bewildered, but she was hurt so bad she was like a child who could not scream or break things. Hyslip knew it was deep inside her, controlled, but yet she was still a child in that she had learned facts without the experience to understand them.

Hyslip said: "What do you want me for . . . to go after him?"

She looked steadily at him, and in the moment he recognized a maturity in her that would bring this thing to understanding in time.

"No," she said. "I wanted to talk to you. I know now you

must have seen this happen before. What should I do now, Webb?"

"Tell your mother. For God's sake, don't tell your father!"

She nodded. "Is that all the advice you have?"

"Bawl your eyes out. Tear hell out of the room."

She looked at him curiously. "What kind of a life have you led that you should know those things?"

He had an impulse to tell her that Starr Purfield's women had sent for him before when Starr's brief interest in them waned. A sudden hatred of Purfield made Hyslip tremble. In the white heat of his emotions was one clear thought: *Kill Starr Purfield.*

Kathleen sat down in a red plush chair. "You can run along to Miss Beasley's now, Webb. I won't bother you any more this evening."

"Kathleen. . . ." He started across the room.

"Go away, Webb."

He stood outside the room a few moments. There was no crying inside. His pistol felt heavy on his thigh. . . .

Starr was telling a story at the wine bar in Madam Beasley's place. He had an appreciative audience. His eyes tightened when he saw Hyslip, but he did not falter in the story. Afterward, in a corner of the room, he said: "It's all over your face, Webb. What did she say?"

Hyslip was cooler now. There seemed to be a touch of humility in Purfield and a sort of mild wonder at himself. He did not laugh. He sat with his legs sprawled out, his youthful face troubled as he stared up at Hyslip.

"I'm just not a settling type, Webb. Let's move on. Let's leave tonight."

"What about Kathleen?"

"Always that, huh?" Purfield grinned. "She'll be all right. She's not hurt."

Hyslip's pistol was in the reception parlor. He picked Starr Purfield out of the chair by his shirt and hit him on the point of the jaw. Purfield went back into the chair. The chair dumped over with his weight, and he lay on the carpet, unmoving.

When Hyslip rode with Kathleen back to Vicuña the next day, she was quieter than usual. Looking at her face, he saw no blight, no deep pain, nor any change except a certain air of thoughtfulness.

"You know why my father has been sending you along, don't you?" she asked.

Hyslip shook his head.

"He's been throwing you at me."

"The hell!" Hyslip stared. "I mean. . . ."

"We laughed about it, Starr and I," she said in an even voice. She looked at Hyslip squarely, as Sidney had when he was considering sending him out to the fence line with Arthur. She put her horse ahead at a trot then, waving Hyslip back when he would have stayed beside her. . . .

Purfield came in from the sawmill one evening two weeks later. He conferred with Sidney about some tools that he needed, and then he came over to where Smallwood and Hyslip were pacing off the site of a new breaking corral.

"See you in a minute, Webb?" There was no mark on Purfield's chin. Nothing about him was changed. "You're going to stick around Vicuña?"

Hyslip nodded.

"Why?"

"For the same reason I gave you there on the Turrets."

That had not been long ago, but it seemed far distant to Hyslip now.

"You and old Bug-Eyes are getting pretty thick, I hear. You're becoming the fair-haired boy. Maybe you figure on winding up top man around here. Is that it?"

"There's a chance."

"Kathleen, too?"

"Leave her out of it, Starr. No need to include her in this."

"You'd be busting up an old friendship, Webb. You're the only man I ever got along with for very long. I've stayed here longer than my time already, but I don't want to leave without you."

He was sincere, Hyslip knew. But was it based on friendship, or a selfish desire to hold onto the only steadying influence there had ever been in his life?

"I'm staying," Hyslip said.

Purfield smiled. "Old Solemn Gus. I wish I could be a little like you. I really do. But nothing holds me for very long. I can't help it, Webb. If I left here without you, it scares me to think of what might happen to me. I'd be in real bad trouble quick, and I know it. You're not going to do that to me, are you?"

"You're the one that's doing it."

"I'll stay a while," Purfield said. "You may get tired of things around here. I mean *everything*, just the way I did." He walked away.

Smallwood came over from where he had stood at the far corner of the corral site. He watched Purfield get on his horse in the yard. "Did you ever hear of the dog in the manger, Webb?"

"I don't think it's exactly like that. He. . . ."

"I do," Smallwood said. "It's damned well exactly that. There goes a man who is no good to himself or to anyone he brushes against. If I thought that him and Kathleen had. . . ." His cold eyes were wicked as he watched Purfield ride away.

Smallwood was thinking the truth, or he would not have mentioned it, Hyslip supposed. It was the memory of black days when he was injured on the Turrets, and days beyond them that made Hyslip say: "I think she's through with Starr, Smallwood."

"Yeah," Smallwood said. "But what brought it about? That's what I'd like to know. Friend or no friend, Webb, don't get in my way if I ever go for Purfield."

Ambrose Sidney was the happiest man at Vicuña; he had made plans, they seemed to be working out, and nothing can please a human being better. He told his wife: "You see what I meant? All she needed was a little encouragement to change over to Webb."

Merva Sidney looked at her husband with wise, pitying eyes. She could not tell him the truth; she could only pray that the days would flow for a long time before he found out the truth, if he ever did.

Now that she had studied Hyslip closely during the evenings he sat with Kathleen in the big living room, Mrs. Sidney had decided that he might, after all, be a good man for Kathleen. If Kathleen did marry Webb Hyslip, it seemed to Merva Sidney that her daughter would be starting her marriage on a mature level.

"Webb ought to laugh more," Sidney said. "He looks younger when he does, and I think Kathleen would like him more. I'll mention that to him."

"Tell him when to breathe, too, Ambrose."

Sidney missed the remark. "The trouble, I think, is Purfield. That fellow has worried Webb to death. I'd fire

Purfield right now if he wasn't so handy at running the saw-mill. Since he got it set up and going, I haven't had to go near the place."

Kathleen came into the room.

Sidney cleared his throat. "No doubt Hyslip will be under-foot again tonight. Why don't you take him riding, or some-thing, to get him out of my sight?"

Kathleen smiled. "I might do that."

I wonder if I had such composure at her age, Mrs. Sidney thought.

Ambrose Sidney rose and started toward an outside door. "I don't want you to get too serious about that fellow, Kathleen. Just because I trust him is no reason anybody else should." The bluster carried into a hollowness that only Sidney was not aware of. He went out smiling.

Kathleen and Mrs. Sidney looked at each other. The smile faded from the daughter's lips. She ran across the room and knelt, putting her face in her mother's lap.

For the first time since discovering what Starr Purfield was, Kathleen gave way to tears. Mrs. Sidney stroked her hair, staring down with troubled eyes.

"I love him so much," Kathleen sobbed. "That's what makes it worse!"

"Starr?" Mrs. Sidney asked gently.

"No. Father, I mean."

It was not the time to ask any questions about Webb Hyslip. "I love your father, too," Mrs. Sidney said. She watched her husband stride across the yard. "We won't tell him anything."

In the middle of the morning Purfield rode in from the sawmill. He talked pleasantly to Sidney about a part for the saw carriage that he wanted to make in the blacksmith shop.

He waved to Smallwood and Hyslip, who were helping on the new corral.

Hyslip was turning to pick up a hammer when he saw the piece of chinking drop from between the logs at the back end of the blacksmith shop. An instant later more chinking fell. Hyslip went over to the shop.

Purfield was pumping the bellows, heating a length of tire iron in the forge. He grinned. "Still hell-bent to be a pioneer on the great Pacheco Grant?"

Hyslip looked through the slot where the line of chinking had been. He could see the road toward Wartrace.

"Who are you expecting, Starr?"

Purfield raised his brows. "Expecting?" He glanced over his shoulder at the slot. "Oh, that! Smoke, son. It goes out through holes, so I made an extra one. Still going to be a pioneer, Webb?"

"I've answered that."

"A man can change his mind. Why, you and me might be fifteen miles east of Wartrace by sundown."

Hyslip chewed his lip. Something in Purfield's grin made him uneasy. Maybe that had always been so. While he was thinking about it, Purfield pushed him off balance with a casual question.

"How's Kate?"

"She's all right."

"Sure she is. No use to glare, Webb. I only asked a civil question. I'm interested in you and Kate. I really am."

Hyslip went back to the corral. His mind was not on his work, and Smallwood eyed him curiously from time to time.

Smallwood was on his way to get a drink of water when Rud Pomeroy, who had been transferred from the fence gang to the sawmill crew, rode in on a lathered horse. He went directly to the blacksmith shop. Smallwood started toward the blacksmith shop, rubbing his hands on his shirt front.

Hyslip was far ahead of him. He stopped in the doorway. Pomeroy and Purfield had been talking, but now they were silent.

"What are you doing over here, Pomeroy?" Hyslip asked.

"He came over to help me," Purfield said.

"He came from the wrong direction," Hyslip said. "He's been in town. He's been on the look-out there." It was clear now to Hyslip, but to the last he did not want to believe what he thought.

"Sure he has." Purfield grinned easily.

Unhurriedly he took his pistol belt from a peg on the wall where he had hung it when he went to work. With his back to Hyslip, he buckled it on. "What do you know! There's somebody coming. Go see where Smallwood is, Pomeroy."

Hyslip said: "Stay right here, Pomeroy."

There was gray in Pomeroy's hair. He had the build of a rough-and-tumble fighter, and he wore a pistol. It was the years behind the grayness that told. He looked from Hyslip to Purfield. "You let me into something, didn't you, Starr?" He walked over to a keg and sat down. "You're the boss, Hyslip."

Smoke from the forge was drifting through the room, but Hyslip could see well enough between the logs, out there to the Wartrace road. The man was on a steeldust. He was tall and stringy. He was Fred Coplon, coming at last.

Matt Smallwood called: "Come out of the shop, you fellows!"

"No shooting," Hyslip said to Purfield.

"Sure. We'll talk him out of it." Purfield laughed.

They went outside. Smallwood had stopped halfway between the watering trough and the blacksmith shop. Pomeroy walked away, going toward the bunkhouse, a man who had lived to get gray by knowing when to leave.

"I'll handle things," Smallwood said.

Purfield walked toward the foreman. Coplon stopped at the meadow gate. He left his horse and ducked through the bars. "Smallwood, I'm coming in to talk to a couple of your men."

"Come ahead." Smallwood did not take his eyes from Purfield. "Don't try a thing, Purfield."

"What makes you think I would?" Purfield raised his hand to rub his cheek slowly. When the hand started down, it went all the way to his pistol.

Matt Smallwood was just as fast. He might even have been a fraction quicker, but he took time for careful aim. Purfield played the main chance, gambling, aiming as one would point a finger. He was ahead. His bullet knocked the little foreman down.

Coplon stopped sixty or seventy feet away.

"Come on, you long drink of water," Purfield said. "Come on in and talk."

"I aim to. Put your pistol away."

"Sure." Purfield slipped his pistol into the holster. "Better saddle up, Webb," he murmured. "Twenty miles east of Wartrace by sundown." He smiled as the tall figure of the marshal came steadily toward him.

Purfield's back was to Hyslip, and that, Hyslip thought, might have been planned with everything else. The Vicuña crew was edging in. Sidney yelled something.

Hyslip drew his pistol. "I'll wreck your arm right at the elbow, Starr."

Purfield watched the marshal. "You wouldn't do that. I know you wouldn't do that." Hyslip's silence was the argument that made Purfield turn. He read Hyslip's face. "What's the matter with you, Webb? You really wouldn't. . . ."

"I'm not bringing trouble," Coplon said. "Hyslip,

Purfield, do you hear me?"

During one long moment that would rise before Hyslip all his life, he saw on Purfield's face everything that had always been there, a selfishness so deep and twisted that it would kill Hyslip before it let him live his own life, and he saw that Purfield knew he had lost, that killing Coplon would not cause Hyslip to run, that the separation had really been up there in the rain and fog on the Turrets.

In a moment stark with loneliness Hyslip recognized these things. He had been Purfield's friend, but Purfield had never known it, for he had always considered Hyslip a symbol of relationship and not a man.

Coplon said something sharply, but it was lost on Hyslip. He saw Purfield start his draw. Hyslip's pistol was in his hand. There was a tick of time for aiming, just a fraction more time than Smallwood had been granted. Hyslip shot once. The tightness went out of Purfield's face. He stared at Hyslip, and then he fell.

There was a numbness then in Hyslip. The hand that held the pistol seemed no part of him. He went forward slowly through the smoke. When he bent over and straightened up again, one thought came and fled. He was thankful that his aim had been deadly, for if it had not been so, if Purfield had lived long enough to talk, he would have grinned and said something that would have added overwhelmingly to the memories.

Fred Coplon walked up. His mouth was a line, and his eyes were impersonal. "I was trying to say that me and the express agent got the charges dropped."

Hyslip fumbled his pistol into the holster. "We heard you say you weren't bringing a fight."

"So?" Coplon looked down at Purfield. "Personal trouble is no affair of mine."

Ambrose Sidney came over from where he had been kneeling by Smallwood. "Some of this is my affair now. One of my foremen got a bullet through the shoulder and now one is dead." He stared at Coplon. "I don't know you, sir, but you're responsible for causing this. I'll hold a trial for you at once."

"Trial?" For once there was slack in Coplon's lips, but his eyes were busy ranging over the Vicuña men all around him.

"Bring him to the porch in ten minutes, Hyslip." Sidney started away.

"He's a United States marshal," Hyslip said. "Don't put on that uniform, Sidney."

"I don't recognize any such office." Sidney swung around. "What was that last you said, Hyslip?"

"Don't put on that uniform!"

Sidney stared at Hyslip, and their wills were locked in combat. Something faded out of Sidney, but it was not his strength; it was rather that he veered suddenly from one driving idea to another. One moment he was stiff with fury, and an instant later he was thoughtful with none of his force diminished, but with an expression that said he himself had finally arrived at a decision he had been long in avoiding.

"The order is revoked," he said, looking at Coplon.

Hyslip went down to the meadow fence. Guppy was out there with the claybanks, and now someone was turning Purfield's blue roan through the bars. It raised its head high, scenting the strangers, and then it trotted over to Guppy, and the two ranged side by side.

On the benches of the Turrets the red and gold of fall had spilled into the aspens. Summer was dying, and it seemed to Hyslip that it happened all at once.

"Come fall, come spring, what's the difference?" Purfield used to say. "Today is the one that counts." There were other expressions, too, and his laugh would echo out of nowhere in the years to come.

After a while Hyslip realized that someone had come up beside him. It was Kathleen. "Are you thinking of leaving, Webb?"

He nodded.

She shook her head. "Don't go away."

They stood there together, and it seemed to Hyslip that they had nothing to say to each other, but still he sensed a strength in their combined presence. He wondered if that was because Purfield had marked both their lives.

"I needed you that night in Wartrace," Kathleen said. "Now you need me."

It was the answer. Time would make it full enough for both of them.

Voices in the Hill

No man, unless it was Riordan Truro, would regret the day of final retreat from collapsing, gloom-soaked drifts and slopes, the abandoning of all the worm-like borings man had made in search of gold in the Midnight Number Three. For fifty years Truro had worked there, scorning offers of supervisory jobs, refusing to be transferred down The Hill to the strictly modern workings of Midnight Number Four or Midnight Number Five.

He was seventy, a squat, powerful man who looked like an enormous frog; the resemblance was startling when you saw him spread on a damp ladder in a raise, his bucket-type carbide lamp rolling darkness imperfectly before him, his brown-mottled face and wide mouth looking up at you. Sometimes miners were startled to hear the ghostly, uneven *poom! poom!* of footsteps coming toward them from liquid blackness unbroken by the gleam that goes with men who work where night is eternal, but Riordan Truro always hailed, booming out his familiar words of greeting and parting— "Keeping your eye on the 'anging wall and look out for the boss!"—and then he would limp into the range of lights.

New miners always asked what ailed his lamp, but veterans of a week or two knew that Riordan Truro moved as surely in the blackness without a light as most men did while carrying one.

"The 'ill dark is a friendly thing," he'd say.

When Brad Traylor, the Midnight general superintendent, called in a promising youngster to send up to Three as a straw boss, he always told the lad: "If you get in a hole or need advice, ask Riordan Truro."

Sometimes the apprentice foremen found Truro in a remote stope where the walls and roof appeared ready to fall at the sound of a loud voice. Sometimes they found him drilling in utter darkness, the measured *clink* of his single-jack coming as an eerie sound. Mostly the lads sought his advice when the crumbling, closing passages in Three threatened to do quickly what The Hill had been doing slowly for three quarters of a century. Riordan's advice was in the form of timbering that held one tiny place while a new threat grew elsewhere. He timbered as if for eternity and then went back to his gleaning, booming as he limped away: "Keeping your eye on the 'anging wall and look out for the boss!"

Literal significance, if any, had long been gone from the words, and perhaps Riordan himself had forgotten that he learned them before he celebrated his eleventh birthday with a twelve-hour shift in a tin mine at Carn Brea, Cornwall. Often young miners, fretting at their detention in dying Three, said Riordan Truro was afraid, that he did every job the long, hard way because of fear he'd never conquered since the day he lay nine hours in darkness in a lonely stope with his foot pinned and crushed by fallen rock.

He limped badly on that foot, mangled one hour after the start of his seventh shift fifty years before. Somehow, in the gloom of weary Number Three, his limp added to the uncanny feeling that he was a misshapen offspring of The Hill itself, that he was in communication with the darkened rock, the blackness, and the dripping water. But in daylight when you saw him in his rose garden, with three Manx cats and two fat old dogs following him, he was just a lame old man with a brown-mottled face and an extraordinarily wide mouth that was always slightly open.

Tren Chambers and Bill Sarson, young, strong, and un-afraid, were two who said openly that Riordan Truro was haunted by fear, that he had never forgotten what The Hill did to his foot, nor the hours he lay when no help came. After one month in Three they were not afraid of squeezing, moving ground, of falling rocks, of loose runs that spill through the crash of broken laggings and fill a tunnel to the roof in the instant that the blast of air snuffs out a carbide flame. Perhaps it was not so much a lack of fear they had but rather lack of respect for The Hill, which for seventy-three years had been moving ponderously, shifting by inches bil-lions of tons of rock along cleavages that no man would ever see, groaning audibly—getting ready without malice to drive one day from its ancient bowels the puny intruders who had made such tiny progress with their steel and dynamite.

The Hill was a patient giant; its white head reared twelve thousand feet, its sloping granite shoulders five miles wide, and its feet set deep in the hot center of the earth. It had never killed or harmed one of the intruders: they had shocked or snuffed the vital spark with their own explosives; they had packed their lungs with drill dust year after year; they had fallen to the bottom of their own burrows; they had crushed their hips between rock walls and overturned tram cars loaded with a ton of muck; in their driving urgency to prick faster at the interior of the giant, they had given their own bodies to be mangled, instead of paying The Hill its rightful due of heavy timber to crush slowly.

The Hill was not at fault; it had always given fair warning;

it had tried not to kill. It had whispered many times: *I am holding these tons of my flesh that you have weakened. I am holding hard, but they are slipping . . . loosening . . . coming down!* When the voice of The Hill was very loud, even fools could hear, but Riordan Truro could hear when the voice was a tiny whisper. He did not curse the part of the giant that was Midnight, Number Three, nor call it a glory hole, Little Siberia, and a death trap, as others did. He said he talked to The Hill. He said so calmly and looked surprised when young men tried to joke about his words. Maybe that is why the young men called him a crazy old fool and felt their backs tingle uneasily when they heard his uneven footsteps coming toward them from the night that is always underground.

Three was dying fast now, but for the last ten years the Midnight Company had kept at least eight or ten men working there, cleaning out little pockets of gold-bearing hematite, following narrow streaks in ancient stopes, gleaning fifteen or twenty sacks of ore a day. It was all hand work. The airline had been pulled away years before. Except in a trifling half mile of the main drift still open, all rails, flanges scalloped from rust, had been removed and piled to rot away in sunlight near the decrepit, empty boiler house. Three's one concession to modernity was a phone in the dry room and a wire that led to Traylor's office on the dump of Five a mile below.

Some miners declared that operations at Three were a result of sentiment, a reluctance on the part of old J. R. Prowers to abandon forever the Midnight property that had founded the fortune he had inherited. Midnight cost accountants knew better. Three was still showing profit. Besides, it was an excellent place to discipline young men who grew too large for their britches down at Four or Five, and it was a cool place to test new miners, putting them under the supervision of a straw boss who himself would be transferred down The Hill after a few months—if he showed any ability at all.

"She can't last much longer," J. R. Prowers told Traylor one day. "Pull the crew in three weeks and shoot the portal down."

"And put old Riordan Truro out of a job?"

"Twenty years ago I gave up trying to make him retire." Prowers looked from the office window up to where the great gray dump of Three blotched the denuded slopes a thousand feet below timberline. "If he won't take a top man's job down here where I can talk to him now and then, he'll have to retire to breeding those bobtailed cats and growing his damned roses."

"Why don't we shut her down today?" Traylor asked. He was thirty-five and looked much older. He was a man who liked to produce ore and the kind of safety records that don't need advertising on a big signboard. Eighteen years before he had started as a tool nipper in Three.

Prowers read his face. "The Hill will hold off as long as Riordan Truro's in it." He looked at Traylor with an expression that warned off possible levity. "Traylor, when Riordan says he talks to The Hill, what he means goes deeper than the understanding that comes from knowing rock, from listening to tommy-knockers and the shift of ground. He senses things, Traylor, that are easy to explain by saying they're damned good guesses. I've seen him stop and look at a roof that had been untimbered for years. He'd say . . . 'Best be catching 'er up!' More than half the time if we didn't . . . down she'd come!"

"He's the kind of miner that's almost extinct now," Traylor said. "After half a century in Three a man should be able to understand. . . ." He paused while a train rumbled from the portal of Five and made the swing toward the dump.

"It's a little deeper than understanding," Prowers said, staring up The Hill toward Three. "When Riordan Truro says the rock talks to him, only a fool will laugh." He rose suddenly and started toward the door. "Shut her down in three weeks." He hesitated. "Three weeks for Three." He went out briskly.

The word spread: in three weeks The Hill could have Three. The last rusted rail would be out and the books could be closed and Riordan Truro could say good bye to the part of The Hill that talked to him.

Tren Chambers and Bill Sarson were glad. In Four and Five were mucking machines, air drills, electric trains, rubber-tired tram cars that needed no track—a chance to do something worthwhile and show their skill. In Three there was dampness, rotting timber, and the feel of finality long overdue.

If Riordan Truro was unhappy about the word, he showed no indication. He went about his work the same as ever, using his light when it suited him, walking without it when he cared to. Going and coming in the main drift, he studied the timbers, sometimes placing the flat of his palm against the wall and standing in an attitude of listening. Maybe he felt the creeping, ponderous power of The Hill, measured day by day and week by week in the mushrooming of caps against the wall, in the bowing of strong posts, in the yielding of heavy mudsills arching up to make little humps in the track.

Anyone could see The Hill was moving in four directions, grinding inward to close its tiny wounds. Such timber as was left was not holding back The Hill; it was merely detaining small slabs, loose rock—little pieces of the patient giant. In one place on a curve six hundred feet inside the main drift the posts against the hanging wall, which happened to be on the outside of the curve, had been sprung by The Hill until the threaded ends of the long hinge pins on the gates of fast-moving loaded cars had ripped for clearance two-inch-deep gouges in the sodden wood.

Riordan Truro pushed his car carefully around this curve, slowing down and swinging the steel box to avoid contact with the timbers. Some of the others followed his example, glancing fearfully at the bowed posts as if they held The Hill itself.

Tren Chambers and Bill Sarson rode their cars out, slowing down for nothing, rocketing around curves, squatting low on the steps, bursting into daylight with a roar.

"You fools are going to knock one of them posts out if you don't slow down!" Joe Bedford, the foreman, said.

Chambers's happy grin sprang from lack of fear of men, devils, or knocked-out posts. "So what, Joe? Maybe we can bring her down before her time is up."

Bedford was as young as Chambers and Sarson and was as tired of Three as they. "Well, take it easy," he said. "We've got only two weeks left. If you bring down the whole country, and someone's left behind you in the hole. . . ."

Sarson laughed. "Grandpa Truro is about the only one who might get caught . . . and he wants to be buried in Three anyway."

"*Wants* to? Hell, he *has* been for fifty years. Talking to the walls!" Chambers's laugh was loud and catching.

"Well, take it easy, you two," Bedford said.

Chambers grinned at Sarson. "Okay, skipper. From now on we'll signal our turns. We'll take the cars apart and *carry* 'em around that curve!"

The two strong and unafraid young men came out faster than ever after that, and so it was no wonder that one day Chambers derailed a car on the narrow curve. He knocked out not one but two posts. Nothing happened except that he leaped over the car and ran twenty feet to get away from an expected cave-in. His heart was pumping hard, and the pit lamp on his hard-boiled hat was whining with new life engendered by the violent shaking it had just received.

He walked back slowly. The wall was just as sound as ever. The caps had not been disturbed. They were tight in their hitches, and their ends were splayed from pressure. Chambers rapped the side of his fist against the taut wood and laughed. His temporary fear was gone. Old sacred ducks like Grandpa Truro probably had puttered years away timbering places like this that needed no support. Dampness would swell any piece of wood and make it tight against the walls. It was no trick for a powerful man to put a derailed car back on the track without assistance. He rode it out full speed.

Joe Bedford was no fool. Three's days were numbered, and he was glad of that, but he went for Riordan Truro. "What do you think, Riordan?"

The squat man raised his light. From years of contact with the crotch of his thumb the hook had produced a calloused ridge. He looked at the pulpy, spreading ends of the caps. He tapped a pick against the wall.

To Joe Bedford the sound was as solid as the certainty of doom.

"Put in two new sets," Riordan Truro said.

"It has to hold only ten days more!"

Chambers and Sarson, on their way out for lunch, stopped to listen, grinning at each other.

"Something tells me she needs two more sets," Riordan said.

"The Hill talking again, pappy?" Chambers asked. "What's the old Hill saying, pappy?"

"Shut up, Tren!" Joe Bedford said. He could laugh with anybody at Riordan Truro when the world was daylight, but in here where faces were gloom-shrouded and shadows rolled on the dank walls and evidence of immeasurable pressure was plain on the battered ends of the caps—laughing didn't come so easily, and Riordan Truro's voice had been so calm and sure.

"Two sets, The 'ill says." Truro dug the flattened end of his lamp hook into a tiny crevice and began to measure with a joint-rusted folding rule so worn that only he could read the figures.

The limping Cornishman put in two new sets, timbering as if he knew the mine would operate another century. He took up rails and put down heavy mudsills; he set and plumbed and fitted new posts under new caps like a cabinet-maker after business. The ends of his head braces bore against the perfect joints of posts and caps squarely and firmly. He put dry, clean-trimmed, close-fitting lagging overhead.

He patted the posts and limped back to some remote part of Three after booming in satisfaction: "Keeping your eye on the 'anging wall and look out for the boss!"

"Wasted three days when he might have been getting out a little ore," Chambers said.

Bill Sarson grinned. "When 'ee was a tiny tyke 'ee talked to 'orses. Now 'ee talks to The 'ill and The 'ill says . . . 'Two sets'!"

Chambers laughed himself red in the face. He walked away, dragging one foot and pulling the corners of his mouth wide with his little fingers. "Keeping your bloody eye on the bloody 'anging wall and looking out for bloody boss!"

A few minutes later Sarson was wondering why he had laughed so hard.

Three days later, when Bedford went down to Four to fill

an opening, Traylor called Chambers into the office and told him to supervise the last rites for Number Three.

"Just ride it out," the superintendent said. "Better figure the last two or three days for pulling track."

Chambers grinned. "We can kick that out in one day with our feet."

Traylor knew that better than Chambers. These kids were all the same, just a-faunching to set a record of some kind. "Ask Truro about anything that puzzles you."

Chambers laughed. "I know. He talks to The Hill and The Hill talks back."

Traylor felt sudden doubt about Chambers. Well . . . he was just a kid and all kids these days were full of smart cracks. "Just ride the week out, Chambers."

The next morning Tren Chambers went up the road rapidly, his mind full of plans about a stope where sloughing walls had exposed a streak of rich hematite that might produce sixty or seventy sacks. He doubted that even Truro had been in the stope since the walls sloughed.

The raise that led to it went up from the main drift approximately eighteen hundred feet in, a compartmented shaft that was cribbed as far as Chambers had climbed, one of the few raises in Three that appeared to be as soundly held as the day it was first timbered. It would be no trick at all to spill the ore down the chute, sack it at the bottom—and who could tell?— if Three wound up with a sudden upsurge in production, word getting around that Tren Chambers had been in charge that last week. . . .

In the dry room Chambers tried to be offhand when he faced his crew of five. He told four of them where to work. He suggested to Riordan Truro that he clean out the stope off the raise eighteen hundred feet in.

"Unh-huh! Unh-huh!" Riordan said. "That's part of an

air shaft that went eight 'undred feet to the surface."

"I know *that!*" Chambers said, having just learned the fact. He saw smiles, smug grimaces that spring when authority gets wet feet. "What's that got to do with it?"

"The 'ill closing off top of raise years ago," Truro said. "Don't want nobody fooling in there."

Expanding smiles made acid etchings deeper in the sensitive skin of authority.

"I want that stope cleaned out!" Chambers said.

Riordan Truro put his old black felt firmly on his head and limped away. He was not flaunting authority; he was only doing what he had done for years.

"I always said you had it up in your neck from fifty years ago!" Tren Chambers cried.

Riorden Truro stopped and looked back in faint surprise. "Me, lad?"

"You! You're scared of that raise!"

Truro half smiled. "Ye're excited, lad." His gaze moved from face to face and only Chambers did not look away. "Git a 'itch on yourself, lad," Truro advised. He went toward the portal, for once forgetting his parting words.

"His guts leaked out that crippled foot," Chambers told the others. He looked at Sarson. "Bill, you clean out that stope."

Sarson stared at the wide flooring. "Sure, Tren . . . if you say, but did you get the look and sound of him when he said The Hill didn't want anybody fooling around up there? Like he actually knew!"

Chambers did not make the same mistake again. He held his temper. He even grinned. "We'll go up together and look it over. If you say it looks too bad. . . ."

Sixty feet above the main drift, the stope led from the

raise, which seemed as solid as a church—tight cribbing, stations in the man-way every sixteen feet. Standing at the small opening into the stope, Chambers felt the weight of darkness overhead. Somewhere between them and the surface, seven hundred and forty feet above, the old air vent was choked solidly, for their lamps burned weakly in the foul air.

Thoughts of what might be hanging in that fluid black square overhead raised the hackles on Chambers's neck, and he wished that the hardheaded, ugly, crippled old relic had kept his mouth shut about The Hill not wanting anybody in this raise. He saw Sarson staring into the oppressive solidness of eternal night, his face already sweating.

Chambers laughed. "You'll get your tonsils knocked loose with a rock, Bill. Let's get in the stope."

The stope was friendly. Although its walls were sloughing, its top was narrowed in a granite arch that had pinched the vein to nothing. In effect, a "horse"—whatever name it went by—had jogged the straight line of the pay streak and left a little body of ore concealed behind the walls where time had exposed it after man had failed.

In spite of having to go down for air every two hours Bill Sarson in one shift sent enough ore down the chute to fill twenty-seven sacks.

Tren Chambers made the daily report casually by phone after shift. "Fifty-three sacks today," he told Traylor. "I just happened to find a little spot that had been overlooked."

"Yeah?" Traylor was not impressed. He had an elbow that didn't open all the way and a leg that still ached at times, both broken when he was learning about little spots that had been overlooked in the days when he was serving time at Three. "Don't get anybody in a jam up there," he said. "You have Truro check that place . . . wherever it is."

Chambers glanced from the corners of his eyes at the men

changing in the dry room, as if they might have heard. That was what you got for making a lousy company money: some big-shot who was a politician got jealous the minute you made a showing.

"All right," Chambers said. Like hell he'd ask old scared-out Riordan Truro anything. Guys like Traylor probably were careful to see that anything good you did never got around to Old Man Prowers.

Down at Five, Traylor put the phone down and looked at J. R. Prowers. "That young Chambers kid knocked out fifty-three sacks at Three this shift."

"They're hell for records, these young squirrels," Prowers said. "Truro will keep him out of trouble, though." He began a story about himself when he was young and full of big ideas.

Traylor heard some of it, but mostly he was thinking how glad he'd be when Three was off his hands.

Riordan Truro seldom volunteered information or advice because most men asked first, but the next morning in the dry room he said: "Chambers, lad, wouldn't be putting nobody up the old raise today."

Chambers grinned. He'd learned that losing his temper over remarks of a doddering, cowardly old man was weakness. "Why not, pappy?" he asked. "Bloody 'ill talking again?"

Nobody smiled. Nobody laughed. Some of them were thinking of Riordan Truro limping without a light in the congealing blackness of The Hill's slowly healing wounds, listening in that darkness—and maybe actually seeing. "New moon last night," Riordan said solemnly.

"New moon!" Chambers lost some of his good nature. The old guy was trying to make a fool of him again.

"There's a superstition among old miners that when the

moon is new cave-ins are at their worst," Sarson explained slowly.

No one in the room knew that, when the moon is new, ground tides sweeping west to east are at their height, loosening, jarring, shifting rock.

But Riordan Truro knew what he knew. "Wouldn't be putting nobody up that raise," he said, and limped away, forgetting for the second straight day his usual parting words.

"Superstitions! About rats leaving the mine! About whistling underground!" Chambers stared around him. "Are you going to let a crazy old Cousin Jack get you down?"

"Don't blow your top, Chambers," someone said. "You're the only one that's excited."

It was afternoon and Chambers was making coffee on the forge when he heard the sound of trouble, the pound of running footsteps near the portal. Men run underground when a breast is grim and bristling with spitted fuses, but they don't run clear to the portal. Chambers's face was gray before the panting miner burst from the timbers.

"Sarson!" the runner gasped. "Trapped! The raise came down!"

"Oh, God!" Tren Chambers cried. That raise, eight hundred feet of it crammed and locked by The Hill—and a man left sealed in a little burrow. "Oh, Jesus Christ!"

"I was sacking ore at the chute when I heard her start. I ran, but when it stopped, I went back and climbed up to Sarson. . . ."

"You climbed up!"

"He was yelling," the miner said. "The stope is blocked with a big chunk wedged in the opening like the devil himself put it there. I talked to Sarson, and he's all right, but in the raise overhead. . . ."

Chambers did not hear. He had the phone and was yelling Traylor's name. Traylor was the man. He'd come up the hard way. He'd know what to do. He had brains. He was decisive. Traylor was the man.

"Get Truro," Traylor said.

Broken timber and huge cold rocks lay where the chute gates and apron had been. Chambers scrambled over the wreckage and looked up. Air was moving coldly around his sweating neck and his lamp was squealing from an updraft. He realized then that air was going clear to the surface, flowing between thousands upon thousands of tons of granite that had broken loose, held now only by its own jam or perhaps by stoppages of timber that might be giving way even as he knelt there. From overhead the *clink* of a single-jack against steel began suddenly.

"Truro!" Chambers called. "Truro! Nothing down!"

He heard a shout, enough to tell him that his signal was acknowledged.

Chambers went up, climbing through smashed timbers and planks from sections of the partition between chute and man-way. The few tons of rocks that had carried clear to the bottom had bounded from side to side, ripping, breaking, tearing some of the ladders into soft splinters. Where he had to climb with his fingers and toes between spaces in the cribbing, the thrust and dig of his nails told him what his eyes had missed: the timber was almost lifeless with dry rot.

He came to Riordan Truro. Squatted like a frog over steel, he was pounding into a grainy mass of pegmatite that almost sealed the entrance to the stope. Through the narrow apertures around the stone, light showed from Sarson's lamp.

"Bill!" Chambers cried. "Are you all right?"

Sarson's voice was a sob. "Get me out of here!"

"We'll get you out!" Chambers's voice was not as steady or reassuring as he would have liked to hear it.

Riordan Truro drilled.

Chambers looked overhead. After a while, just where his light was losing its unequal fight with darkness, he saw the brutal planes of heavy rocks thrusting through a tangled block of ancient timber. The Hill was probing a finger deeply into a freshly opened wound, holding it steady for a moment only by caprice. He looked at the huge stone blocking the stope. No power on earth was going to get it out of there until it had been broken.

Chambers held his voice low for only Truro to hear. "A shot might bring down everything."

Clink! The drill bit deeper. It was pointed toward the center of the granite rock where a stick of dynamite would be enough to break the stone into large chunks. *Clink!*

"I know," Riordan Truro said.

And so did Tren Chambers. Sarson had a meager chance. He looked above. Or any man who stayed long in this raise.

A sob cut Bill Sarson's cry in half. "Get me out . . . of here!" He was eighteen and had planned to go that night to a dance.

"You'll be getting out, lad!" Riordan Truro said.

Tiny rocks fell from the jam above. Chambers cringed and held his breath as they rattled on his safety hat. Somewhere deep in The Hill tommy-knockers rapped.

Bill Sarson began to pray. "Jesus, tender shepherd, hear me . . . Jesus, tender shepherd, hear me. . . ." That was all he could remember, so he said it over and over in the voice of a little boy, with sobs breaking over his words.

"Let me. . . ." A rock the size of a man's fist struck the edge of Chambers's hat and knocked it off. He heard his lamp whistling in outrage, and then hat and lamp were bumping down the raise.

The *clinks* stopped for a moment. Light from the hissing tongue of Truro's ancient lamp showed blood streaming from the driller's left hand. Riordan Truro spread and clenched his fingers.

"The 'ill don't like it!" he said, and began to drill again.

"Jesus, tender shepherd, hear . . . get me out of here!" young Sarson screamed.

Clink! "Easy, laddie!" *Clink!*

Somewhere in the awful murk above them The Hill could hold no longer. The muffled thump of rock and crashing wood came close and closer.

Tren Chambers put his strong, wide hands over his head and huddled against the foot wall. "Oh, God!" he cried.

Rocks thumped and knocked and settled sullenly, and a barrier was created somewhere between this pit of hell and yellow sunlight lying warmly on gray slopes almost a thousand feet above, stopped and held a hundred tons of granite, and let three terror-stricken men breathe air and life a little longer.

Clink! The drilling had not faltered by a stroke.

Overhead a timber popped, and little rocks came down and loose granite ground against loose granite with awesome, shuddering sounds. The updraft became a rush. The jet of flame on the spout-like burner of Riordan Truro's lamp bent upward, squealed, and died.

The dark pressed in and put soft crushing fingers on young Tren Chambers. The hammer never missed a stroke.

"Jesus, tender shepherd, hear me . . . get me out of here!" Bill Sarson screamed. His lamp was out, and he was a little boy trapped by clutching darkness, all the darkness that little boys have feared for centuries.

The Hill moaned and little rocks went swishing past Tren Chambers, pressed against the wall.

Riordan Truro spoke between hammer blows. "Easy, lad. Drills, Chambers. Powder. Long rope. Clear the chute."

"It's dark . . . I can't see to move . . . I'm afraid. . . ."

"Take my lamp," the driller said.

The wall was comforting, an anchor and a friend, but Chambers left it and took two steps along the sodden plank that ran along the foot wall. His trembling fingers touched the hook of Truro's lamp, hanging from the timbers. They knocked it loose. It fell and bumped and came to rest sixty feet below.

"Candles in my jumper," Truro said. He drilled.

Men were calling from below, but Chambers could not identify the words. He heard the terror in himself, the whisper of The Hill, the hammer blows, and the childish, whimpering entreaties of Bill Sarson: "You'll get me out, won't you, Riordan? You'll get me out, won't you . . . ?"

"Sure, laddie!" Riordan said. *Clink!* "Sure, laddie!"

Beneath the rhythmic movements of Riordan's elbow, Chambers found a pocket. His fingers touched the cold, misshapen stubs of candles long carried there. Three matches brought a light that held until he saw the first steps he must take.

Twice more the candle helped for an instant, so comforting, so feeble in the very bowels of gloom where death was whispering. Above he heard the never-ending *clink* of steel, and courage began to come from it and from thoughts of that crippled old Cornishman who knelt and drilled to save a life.

Chambers dropped at last where three silent, pale miners waited. All knew what hung overhead but only the third had seen, so Chambers sent him out to get what Truro wanted.

The other two he took with him to clear the chute of wedged timber and planks.

"What for?" one asked. "Bill ain't hurt, is he?"

"Clear it!" Chambers said savagely. "Truro said to!"

Their lamps guttered and whined and went out, but they kept relighting them and working, reaching through the broken partition from the man-way until the chute was clear.

The drilling never stopped.

Steel bound with rope, the line over his shoulder, an armed stick of dynamite in his jumper pocket, Chambers went up in the dark after the third miner returned. He held a match shielded in his hands and saw that Truro had put the starter drill down within an inch of the head, turning it with fingers that were dark with blood.

Rocks pattered on Chambers's back and shoulders, but The Hill was holding while it could.

"All right, Bill?" Chambers called.

" 'Ee's getting 'is dust spoon for me," Truro said.

The driller already had a dust spoon, Chambers knew, an iron rod lipped and cupped on one end for lifting drillings from a dry hole. Scrabbling sounds came from the stope, and Sarson called: "Here it is!" Chambers heard the ticking of iron against rock and knew that Sarson was thrusting his dust spoon toward Riordan Truro.

"Good lad!" Truro said.

A moment later Sarson's voice held the terror that action had taken from his mind for at least a little time. "Hurry, Riordan!" he cried. "Hurry . . . won't you hurry?"

"You'll be at the dance tonight," Riordan said. *Clink!* his hammer said with a higher pitch on longer steel. "Make fast the rope, Chambers, lad."

Chambers obeyed, and then with nothing to do but wait

he felt once more the throttling spell of darkness and death poised above.

Truro seemed to know. "Go down!" he ordered.

Chambers went down. He was there when electric lanterns bored the dark, when Prowers and Traylor, followed by two lads with a first-aid case and stretcher, came up the drift and joined the other waiting men.

They listened without comment to Chambers's story.

"I'll take a look," Traylor said.

"You will like hell!" Prowers said. "Stay down."

They waited. The first-aid lads sat down and smoked. The Hill was hushed. Only the *clink* of steel disturbed it—and the sound of Riordan Truro's voice calling encouragement to Sarson now and then.

Oh, God, Chambers prayed silently, *let them come down that raise to walk in the sunshine again.*

They were tensed when the sound of drilling stopped. Moments later Truro's call came hollowly: "Fire!"

Stepping back with the others, Chambers thought there was only one place he could go to get in the clear. Sarson could go to the back of the stope, but Riordan Truro would have to climb in darkness . . . up, up toward that brutal, pointing finger.

The explosion was hollow with the sound of deep, clean breakage. Big chunks of granite roared down the chute and leaped against the tunnel wall to fill the drift with the sharp coppery smell of bruised rock.

They heard Riordan's booming voice: "Stand clear!"

More fragments came and jarred against the wall and lay sullenly on the tunnel floor.

And then Riordan called: "Man down!"

Torches played up the chute. Men knelt and stared at a limp body dangling toward them.

"The shot . . . ?" one of the first-aid lads asked.

"Shot, hell!" Prowers said. "He could have set on that rock and never got hurt, the way Riordan Truro handles powder. You kids have never seen the way a trapped, scared man comes out of a hole when it's finally opened!"

They received Bill Sarson and put him on the stretcher.

Chambers grabbed an electric lamp and leaped back to play it up the chute. He saw a shadowy, frog-like figure walking down the wall. He steadied the light and stared, and his spine tingled. Even after Chambers realized that Truro was holding the rope in both hands and using his feet against the wall, it still appeared that the man was walking without support.

Chambers heard no sound of moving ground; not even a tiny rock fell. The Hill was deathly still, but Riordan Truro yelled suddenly, "Get out! Get out!"

He came another twenty feet before Chambers heard. The Hill had held as long as it could, even for Riordan Truro. Everything above came free.

Truro slid another ten feet and then let go. The Hill was coming then, sending its own hard flesh to fill forever this pin prick of a shaft, four by nine, eight hundred feet deep. The giant thundered and moaned and maybe the last was because a friend who knew and loved The Hill was in the way.

Truro's crippled foot went under him and turned when he landed. His weight came down hard but not all the way, for Tren Chambers, young, strong, and unafraid, but no longer in arrogance, was there to grab and hold. He staggered back to safety with Riordan Truro in his arms.

The Hill roared down and sealed up its scar. Rock moved and groaned along distant cleavages that no man would ever see, and small rocks began to tumble in the main draft.

"Let's go!" Prowers cried. "Head for daylight!"

They went, the young, clean first-aid lads carrying Sarson. He had the bruise mark of a drill on his head, inflicted when Truro had caught him by the shirt in utter darkness and struck just hard enough to knock him senseless and keep him from diving head first down the chute. Chambers was last, carrying Riordan Truro in his arms. The old man's crippled foot was bruised and swelling and pained enough to make a saint cry out in agony. "I tried not to 'it the lad too 'ard," he said.

"He's all right," Prowers said. "I hear him grunting now. He's faking to get a free ride out."

Those who had not respected The Hill were not yet through with it. Slabs and coffin lids that had been slipping from its grasp for years had been jarred and jolted by tremors from the caving raise. They sloughed, they fell with sullen chunking thumps. It seemed that the whole passage was coming in and down. One place was like another, and yet The Hill would have crushed the intruders. Rocks fell ahead; they fell behind; they fell when men had passed. A miner carrying the first-aid case held it tightly. It had a cross upon it.

Then somewhere ahead tortured timber broke, spilling rock and fear into the drift. The stretcher-bearers stopped where no rock had fallen, where the drift was clear with bright wood chips showing. The others caught up and joined the two, all waiting under timbers that Riordan Truro had set a few days before. They were still six hundred feet from daylight.

"The old girl's acting up a bit," Prowers said. He flashed his light on Truro. "All right, young fellow!" He grinned. "A rock may fall here and there . . . but The Hill knows you're still inside!"

I hope it does, I hope to God it does! Traylor thought.

The first-aid lads looked down a drift where slabs were

spilling from their ancient, weary bearings. The drift was a horrible death trap, a waiting, leering thing ready to grind flesh and bones against rusty rails.

Riordan Truro had his hand upon the wall. When it seemed that rocks were falling worse than ever, he said: "Go now!"

The stretcher-bearers hesitated.

"Move! You heard him!" Chambers roared.

Bill Sarson came to and screamed: "Don't leave me in all this dark! You'll get me out, won't you, Riordan?" He thought he was still in the stope, but his words expressed the thoughts of men behind him.

They went on, up and over cave-ins, slipping on talc-slicked granite slabs, hunching their shoulders at the sound of every thud.

They came at last to daylight.

They helped Sarson to his feet. He staggered in the sunshine and tried to clutch it to his breast. "I'm out! I'm out!" he cried.

The first-aid men fussed with Truro, removing his boot, probing at his swollen foot. They exchanged quick glances when they saw the extent of the terrible injury he had borne and walked upon for half a century.

Tren Chambers wept unashamedly as he knelt by Truro and took his hand. "For what I said . . . and the things I did. . . ."

Riordan Truro's wide mouth smiled. "Good lad!" he said.

Walking out on the dump so that no one could see the trembling of his hands as he filled and lit his pipe, Prowers looked far up the gray slopes, past where the last twisted trees grew, to where the white crown of the patient giant gleamed brightly in the sun.

"You did hold off, didn't you?" he murmured.

A little later he scowled when he saw Tren Chambers changing clothes in the dry room.

"Where do you think *you're* going in the middle of a shift?" Prowers demanded.

Chambers stared. "I'm through." He was merely stating a fact that anyone should know.

"Who never made a mistake?" Prowers growled. "I made one today when I rode up with those two young fools that think wagons are mountain goats. You get that crew busy and have Three's portal shut down for good by quitting time!"

Chambers stood up.

Prowers's voice was still a growl. "When you learn something about fear and get a touch of humility as young as you are . . . it's early enough to do you some good. Now get to work!"

He walked out of the dry room.

The first-aid lads were carrying Riordan Truro toward the wagon. "Keeping your eye on the 'anging wall and look out for the boss!" he boomed.

Ride the Wild Trail

1

Scarcely an hour after breakfast, Wyatt Monroe dropped the harness he was mending and stared with a breachy expression through the manure window on a land where spring was flowing all green and blue and yellow, with the wondrous distance of Texas running into the forever. The sight twisted a strange dissatisfaction in Wyatt Monroe whose family called him Stub—for "Stubborn."

After a time he picked up a piece of breeching and examined it moodily. The leather was well-oiled. One side of it was glazed from long rubbing against Sam Monroe's horses, but the other side was scarred with age cracks that opened and closed as Stub bent the leather in his hands.

The breeching offended him. He hurled it against the back of the workbench where it upset a can of rivets, crusty with verdigris. They spilled across the bench as Stub flung himself around and strode out of the barn. Outside, spring held him in warm, gentle hands. He stared at the sky, trying to fathom the blue depths of it, reaching and wondering until a roiling discontent jerked him away.

He was going toward the house when he saw dust smoke on the prairie, thin mist staining the horizon, wavering above a white-topped wagon headed north. It was early—the grass was not yet a month high—but Stub squinted hard and knew what he saw, a cook wagon, forerunner of a drive going beyond the distant Red, up where the Yankees clamored to buy longhorns that were not worth fifty cents a head here.

The wagon dipping into vastness increased Stub's feeling of rebellion against his own puttering life. The sap was up in him, and he was full of energy for some things, and he did not know what to do about it. He was a high-cut figure. All the Monroes were big-boned and strong with rawhide muscles, and most of them, like Stub, were freckled. His hair was a stubborn, sandy color. His blue eyes smoked with a nameless discontent.

Dust on the prairie. He wondered where the wagon would camp tonight. Suddenly the speculation meant nothing. To hell with the wagon. He went on toward the house. His mother and his six sisters had left at sunup to visit at the Weldon place and see Mrs. Weldon's triplet girls, born two weeks ago. Thirteen kids in the Monroe family. A man would think they could stay home and look at each other, instead of high-tailing twenty miles just to see three new babies.

Pa and the Monroe boys were out beyond the west lake somewhere, plowing and building fence, and maybe Pa and Randall, Stub's oldest brother, were scouting around for cattle. Pa didn't know what he was, a farmer or a cowman, in Stub's opinion.

The room where the Monroe males slept was in fine disorder, which did not bother Stub, except that it took him longer to find Mike's pistol. Once it had been Stub's pistol, but he had traded it to his brother for a Walker Colt. The details of that transaction still rankled. Stub had his own caps, powder, and lead.

He went to the east lake for shooting practice. Between loadings he watched the great pall of dust that was coming on the trail of the wagon. The first drive of the year. It looked like a big one. After a time the rocking crash of the pistol, the buck of it in his hand, and the shards of wood flying from the target board began to soothe Stub. Soon he forgot all about the harness.

He was aiming with both eyes open and the pistol held easily in his hand, when Pa said: "You're a fair shot, Stub."

Stub whirled around. "Why, sure."

Pa was a big man, dark-faced, with startling blue eyes. His thick beard covered his collar and the first two buttons of his shirt. He stood with his hands clasped before him, rocking gently on his toes, with a slight smile on his face.

"I've no objections to shooting practice," Pa said, "except that I told you to fix that harness."

"I'll get it done."

"Yes, you will."

Pa's quiet assurance started the rebellion in Stub again. He just naturally didn't take kindly to any kind of correction, even if he was a mite afraid of Sant Monroe.

"If you'd let me go with the others, instead of sweating over a miserable pile of worn-out leather in a barn, then maybe I'd. . . ."

"You had four fights with your brothers in two days," Pa said. He frowned as if he could not quite understand it. "And now you're headed for another with Mike over using his pistol without permission. I think. . . ."

"I got cheated out of that pistol in the first place." Stub's voice quivered with excitement. "I guess, by God. . . ."

"Watch your tongue, there," Pa said quietly. "Give me that pistol, and then get back to work."

Work! Greasy, beat-up leather that kept falling apart. It was all a waste of time when a man could be doing something that counted, something that would show everybody, especially Pa, that he was a man.

Pa stepped forward. "Give me the pistol, Wyatt."

Stub was surprised to hear himself say: "I guess you'll have to take it the hard way."

Pa said nothing. He merely took the pistol away. Sitting in mud at the edge of the lake, Stub wondered how it had happened so fast. His arm was hurting, he had been belted in the jaw, and here he was on his hind end with Pa standing over him, not in the least excited.

"Why do you always argue?" Pa asked. "You're the worst of the whole tribe for mule-headed arguments. Come on."

They went back to the house together. Stub's hard shock of surprise flowed into anger. He was a man, and he'd been treated like a kid. His rebellion was a knotted sore inside him. Pa's buckskin and Hilb, Randall's blue roan, were standing in the yard. Stub looked around for Randall. Just let *him* open his mouth now. . . . But Randall was not around, and then Stub realized that he was building a fence and had asked Pa to bring the blue roan in so it wouldn't have to stand in the hot sun until noon. Randall was mighty particular about his horse. The thought was another gust of fury through Stub.

Pa gave Stub the pistol. "Clean it and put it back where you found it. I want that harness mended so I can use it in the morning. Tomorrow you can stay home and fix another set." Pa led the blue roan into the barn.

Stub balanced the pistol as he watched his father walk away. He stared his revolt sullenly, but all the time he knew he was going to obey, and the thought seemed to make him less of a man and that troubled him most. Pa was still around when Stub came from the house, after cleaning the pistol. He watched Stub with a troubled expression and seemed to be on the verge of speaking, but his son stalked past him to the barn.

The dust cloud was now in line with the manure window.

Pa came in and stood by the workbench, absently picking up the scattered rivets and dropping them back into the can. "A man's got to have discipline, Stub, but, even so, it's seldom you ever see me lay a hand on one of you boys."

Stub slammed a rivet hole through the breeching and threw the punch against the back of the bench with a *clang*.

"A family like ours . . . there's bound to be quarrels and fights," Pa said. "But lately you're battling with everybody all the time. I used to laugh at your stubbornness, but now it's beginning to worry me, boy. You don't take any correction a-tall. You're a man now, Stub, so. . . ."

"Treat me like one, then."

Pa looked out on the dust. He seemed to be thinking away back to something, mustering vast patience. His beard rustled as he rubbed it slowly. "You've got to start acting like one, too."

"Like my brothers, huh? Yes sir, yes sir, every time you open your mouth."

Pa's look was mild, but his voice took an edge. "I figure for my boys to mind me, Stub. You're one of them."

"I'm damned tired of minding you!"

Sant Munroe sighed. "I've seen that, no matter how I've tried to handle you. But as long as you're here, you'll just have to mind me. I don't try. . . ."

"I can leave, I guess."

"You could." Pa nodded. "But you ain't learned enough at home to leave just yet. You got a chip on your shoulder. Around here, you get it knocked off with fists. Somewhere else, you wouldn't be anybody's brother, Wyatt. Folks wouldn't be particular how they took that chip off your shoulder. So I guess you'd best stay a while."

"The hell you say." Stub took a knife from the tool rack

and sliced the breeching in two, and then he looked directly at his father, and then quickly away.

Sant Monroe was completely still, a sort of hurt expression in his eyes. "I came here to try to talk some sense into you, but it never works. Now I guess I'll have to talk to you by hand."

Stub was ready. He grabbed a handsaw from a peg. Holding it in both hands, he drove it out and down. The teeth raked into Pa's beard, dragging whiskers with them until the saw was fouled and stuck. Pa's head jerked forward, and he let out a mighty groan of pain. Stub let go of the saw and tried to slide away to the door, but his father kicked his feet out from under him.

Pa's eyes were full of water, and he was working his jaw like a fish. "God A'mighty," he muttered, rubbing whiskers with both hands. "Get up."

Blinking water from his eyes, Pa backed Stub to the wall, crowding in remorselessly. Stub did not care about running now. His eyes blazed. The first savage outburst of his rebellion had given him courage to stand and fight.

Suddenly Pa stopped. He wore a puzzled expression. "Son," he said, "what the hell is the matter with you?" He stood there, not indecisive, but bearing tremendous patience on the thought that a beating would not straighten out the problem.

He's afraid of me! Stub thought. He hit his father in the jaw. Sant Munroe grunted. He tried to smother Stub's arms. Stub ground his heel down on his father's instep, and then tried to knee him.

That was the last of the first phase of the fight. Stub never knew what happened. He woke up, lying by the water trough, with his father standing over him. Soaked with water, with his brain befogged, Stub twisted around until he got both hands on the water trough and forced himself up. His father still wore a puzzled expression.

"I can't quite make you out, Stub. If you. . . ."

"I make you out all right," Stub said. He lurched forward and took a swing at Pa. That was the last of the fight.

The second time Stub was longer getting his senses back. He was sitting on the edge of the trough, holding his head, when Pa said: "You bring these things on yourself, Stub. Mend the harness. I want it tomorrow." He limped a little as he walked to his horse.

Stub watched him ride away, hating the sight of him, hating the inexorable patience of him, writhing the more because of Pa's quiet assumption that he would be obeyed. He did not try to move until Sant Monroe was a mile away.

As he staggered toward the barn, the dust cloud caught Stub's attention again. He stopped. All his bitterness took shape and made a plan.

Fifteen minutes later he rode away on Randall's blue roan, in his father's best saddle. It was an honest rig from the days when Pa had been a cowboy. The horn was broad, the leather heavy, and the *tapaderos* showed the marks of much brush work. Behind Stub was a blanket roll, covered with a section of a brand-new wagon sheet he had ripped. He was wearing Jeff's boots, fine Spanish leather, beautifully stitched, with soles so thin you could count the rattles of a dead snake by stepping on them and wiggling your toes a little. He had on Roark's gloves. They were gauntlet style, with C.S.A. stitched in faded gold on the cuffs. The pistol belt and scabbard belonged to Bradford, but the pistol, oddly, was Stub's. He could not have explained why he had taken it in preference to the one he had traded for it. But in the back of his mind was a wish to get revenge on someone for the trick that had been played on him with the Walker Colt. The oiled cedar butt grips that he had made himself were warm to his hand as he tested to be sure that a rawhide thong running in a strange manner clear through the holster was still secure. Under his shirt was a slab of cornbread he had grabbed on his way through the kitchen.

Stub Monroe was on his way to meet the world. His physical equipment was good. His mind was bitter.

11

It took him an hour to swing wide around the herd. He crossed a trail pounded a hundred yards wide, where the odor of dust still hung in the air. At noon he was munching cornbread as he squatted in the grass a mile on the east flank of the drive. He watched the herd drift up slowly to the wagon. The cowboys ate. The wagon went out ahead once more, and then the longhorns made their slow smoke northward.

The loneliness of a bunch-quitter came to Stub, and it made him all the more embittered. There was a way to gain a place with the drivers of the herd, and that was to fight his way in, to show them that he was as tough as any of them.

But he could not go in at once. Pa would be along, and Randall, and maybe other Monroes, checking to see if he had joined the drive. Pa had said Stub was not smart enough to leave home. Pa could go to hell. But still Stub was not going to tangle with him again and test the point. He would wait three days, and by then the Monroes would have to figure he had gone somewhere else besides with this drive.

Stub paced the flank of the drive like a buffalo wolf. He felt like one. His family had made an outcast of him. At sunset the remuda whirled ahead and passed the wagon where it had stopped on Comanche Creek. The drivers brought the herd in slowly, letting it spread out to graze. After dark the cook's fire was a bright spot that kept reminding Stub of biscuits and beef and coffee.

In the thick layers of the night came the lonely sound of cowboys, singing as they rode the edges of the bedded herd. Hilb was restless on his picket rope. Once Stub raised on his elbows and cursed the horse. "You're not going home, damn you!"

Hungrier than a rawhider, Stub was up at dawn. He ate the rest of his cornbread and watched the camp break. The herd moved out reluctantly. With a sullen sort of wonder Stub saw the drive get underway. He was not part of it yet, and he had no other place to go. His lips curled at the thought of his brothers, stuffed with breakfast, nodding or saying yes to Pa as he gave them orders.

For two days and nights Stub held out. His hunger was a growing pain. Alternately he placed the cause of it on his father or on the drivers of the herd. Before noon he went in.

The remuda was in charge of a dark youth with the beadiest eyes Stub had ever seen. Scorpion eyes. A ragged, insolent-looking kid who was possibly two or three years younger than Stub.

"Where's your damned trail boss?" Stub asked.

The youth spat dust. He looked at the gauntlets, at Stub's frayed hat, and the look was a sneer. "You expecting to find him back here?"

Stub shoved Hilb in against the kid's grulla. The blue roan was two hands taller than the hairy pony. "I asked you a question, button."

"Button! I suppose. . . ." The kid gave Stub a curious stare, and then the scorpion eyes wavered and broke. Stub took a savage pleasure from it, a feeling of power that he had never experienced.

"The boss is on point." The remuda driver slid a quick

look across Stub's features. There was no respect in it, but there was fear and hate.

"My name's Nueces," Stub said. "I'll be around." He rode into the deep dust of the drag.

A sweating man in a faded blue flannel shirt turned his head to look as Stub came up on his right side. The cowboy's eyes were small and squinty, his forehead and cheeks glossed with yellow dust. A red bandanna masked his face from the bridge of his nose down.

"Where's the boss?" Stub asked.

The man stared at Stub's rig. He looked the blue roan over silently.

"Did you hear what I said?" Stub said.

The cowboy's tiny eyes glinted. He pulled the bandanna down. The lower part of his face was plump and red, and he had a slash mouth like a frog. "Yeah, I heard you." He studied Stub some more. Now that the man's face was all in one piece, what had seemed like an evil sparkle in his eyes was more nearly wicked humor.

"My name's Nueces," Stub said. "I figure to catch on with this drive."

"That's interesting. I'm Bull Foot."

"Where at is the boss?"

"Kinard?" Bull Foot grinned from ear to ear. "On the point somewheres, I reckon."

Stub peered through the dust at the wallowing backs of cows, at the jerky movements of peak-rumped laggers in the drag. "Sort of a mixed bunch."

"Sure is." Bull Foot grinned again at some humor of his own.

"What's the big joke?"

Bull Foot looked innocent. He pulled his bandanna up once more and said something that Stub could not make out.

Stub suspicioned that he had been insulted, or at least laughed at. He was of a mind to jerk Bull Foot's neckerchief down, but, instead, he stiffened his back and rode on. There would be time to make a believer out of Bull Foot later on.

As Hilb topped a little rise, Stub had a good view of the herd, shaken down now into good marching pace, a great living mass that pushed slowly ahead under a haze that took a golden color from the sun. He saw men on swing make easy sallies to crowd strays back into line.

Far ahead on point a man on a buckskin with dark legs sent his horse shouldering toward a big steer dribbling out from the edge of the drive. The steer lowered its head and tried to hook away from the horse, and for a moment it appeared that the two animals would crash belly-up, but the steer moved away suddenly and rocketed back into the herd with its tail high.

The movements of the buckskin had been so deft and effortless that Stub decided the rider must be Kinard. To hell with him, boss or no boss, he was just another man.

He quartered off the rise and rode toward a cowboy on a wiry blood bay. The rider saw him and waved him back. Stub rode on, anyway. He saw the cowboy's right hand move in a blur. Something glinted through the dusty air and disappeared into the grass. The man was off his horse and back into the saddle in a moment. He wiped a knife across the rump of the bay and gave Stub a challenging stare.

"What the hell was the idea of crowding up on me like that when I signaled you to hold off?"

Stub saw a rattler writhing and humping near a hole. Its head had been severed. When he looked again at the cowboy, the knife was out of sight. The man's eyes were a cold yellow, like winter dust. His black beard grew in tight ringlets.

"My name's Nueces. . . ."

"Don't ever crowd in on me, kid, when I wave you back."

Kid! The word pulled a trigger in Stub's brain. His stomach growled with hunger. The dust was hurting his eyes. This man was trying to give him orders.

"You the boss?" Stub asked. The man did not answer, so Stub said: "I ain't used to paying mind to stray riders waving their arms around at nothing."

"By God!" the cowboy said. "What salt lick did you crawl out of? I've got a notion to. . . ."

"You better get another one," Stub said. "I hung a handsaw in the last beard I saw like yours." He rode on, but he could not keep from glancing back. The bearded man was staring at him. Stub touched the handle of his Walker and kept on riding.

And now—Kinard. Stub felt that he had pretty well established himself so far. Kinard was just another man. But still Stub felt a rising tightness in his chest. This next step was the important one. He watched the way Kinard rode, not slouching, not stiffly, but with a wiry ease that fitted the motion of his horse. He was wearing a hat that was dipped forward like the handle of a drinking gourd.

Stub trotted Hilb up to him. "You Kinard?"

The man turned to look at Stub. His manner was so deliberate, his narrow gray eyes so insolent and searching, that Stub felt the familiar gorge of anger choking up. After a moment the man nodded. His nose was thin and sharp. He had a mean, tight jaw and thin lips.

He looked like a son-of-a-bitch, Stub decided. "My name's Nueces. I'm. . . ."

"What were you jawing about back there with Curley Volland?" Kinard's voice was sharp.

"The one on the blood bay?"

"Yes."

"Nothing much. He tried to get flip with me."

Kinard looked coldly at Stub's pistol, at his rig, at Hilb's high, powerful lines, at the gauntlets. His manner, like that of the scorpion-eyed kid with the remuda, was insulting, but there was a high degree of careless assurance in it that Stub did not care to buck. He began to hate Kinard right there.

"I'm looking for a job with this lay-out," Stub said.

"The answer is no." Kinard drove ahead quickly and ran a big red roan steer back into the herd. He did not bother to glance at Stub again until Stub trotted Hilb beside the buckskin once more. "Go home before your old man catches up with you and beats three kinds of hell out of you."

"I said I was looking for a job, Kinard."

"Not with me you ain't. Beat it."

"Has my father talked to you?"

"It wouldn't make any difference whether he had or not," Kinard said. "I don't need you."

Stub looked at the thousands of pale horns swinging in the pall of dust, at the flowing backs and tossing heads. The sounds of shuffling hoofs, the clacking of horns, blended with the sight, the odors, the motion, and the sheer bigness of the drive.

For a moment the spectacle caught at a longing in Stub. This was the noise and the action that he had wanted. This was life, going up the trail, headed north beyond mysterious rivers. And then the old rebellious spirit gnawed him. Kinard was trying to deny him what he wanted. Kinard, like Pa, was trying to stand in his way.

"I say you need another man."

"Do you?" The trail boss gave Stub a brief look. "What was that name again?"

"Nueces Monroe." Stub's hopes rose.

"I don't need you, Nueces Monroe," Kinard said flatly.

Smoking with fury, Stub whirled the blue roan and rode back along the herd. Curley Volland was flipping his knife. His mouth was small and secret. He gave Stub a twisted grin and said: "I might consider a little trading for that Walker you got there, before you drag yourself home."

"I'm not a damned bit interested, and who said I was dragging myself back home?"

"A little bird left the tracks all over your face." Volland laughed. "You wouldn't have lasted long with this outfit if Kinard had been fool enough to take you on."

Stub was bitter enough to crowd in and take a poke at Volland, but he watched the man flip his knife and decided he couldn't do much about Curley at the moment.

When Stub got back to where he was, Bull Foot studied Stub's expression. He lowered his bandanna. "Too bad, kid, but maybe it's a good thing, after all. This ain't no life for a young, ambitious man. I been at it quite a spell, but this is my last drive. I'm getting me a job up North where there ain't nothing to do but sort of ride around a little pasture between hills. No thousand miles of eating dust and getting tromped and drowned in rivers and things like that. I'm going to settle where you get three meals a day all the time and go to town once a week. This just ain't no life for a young, ambitious fellow. I. . . ."

"Whose turn is it to rustle for the cook?"

"I. . . ." Bull Foot opened and closed his huge mouth. "Jinglebob's." He jerked his head toward the cavvy. "It won't do you any good."

"I didn't ask you."

"Being proddy as a bogged cow won't do you any good, either, and you didn't ask me that." Bull Foot jerked his bandanna over his nose and mouth.

★ ★ ★ ★ ★

Stub angled back from the drag until rolling hills lay between him and the herd. He rode west like a demon, and then he swung north with the line of the drive. The cook was digging his fire trench, pausing now and then to make sour appraisal of a veering wind. Stub raced in on the camp with a bundle of firewood on the end of his reata.

The cook eyed the wood critically. "Who the hell are you?"

"Nueces Monroe." Stub rode by the wagon and grabbed a bucket. He raced to the creek and came back, galloping, and he did not spill much water, all of which the cook accepted as a matter of course.

The cook's name was Cinches. He did not give his last name. He did not look like an old man, but he acted like one, walking toed-in with little steps, eyeing the ground as if for holes. He was a tall man with a turkey-gobbler neck. Instead of a sack he wore an old leather blacksmith's apron that looked as if it had the grease of a thousand meals soaked in it.

"First time up the trail, huh?" he asked.

Stub nodded curtly.

"You'll find out. You'll see. I been up this trail from when she started, and before that I drove hides to the coast. Look at me now, cooking for a bunch of savages. I know a widow that runs a boarding house in Caldwell where we're going. Always wanting to marry up with me. This time I'm taking her on. I'll do my cooking on a stove, and them that bellyache about it, I'll by God throw out the door without opening it. Get some more water."

Stub got the water. He rustled more wood than needed. He tried to make himself useful, and all the while he kept one eye on the herd coming slowly toward the camp.

Jinglebob came in with the remuda. He watered the horses

at the creek and stayed away from the wagon after he saw that the chores were done. Cinches was frying steaks from a yearling butchered that morning. He kept talking about his busted bones and rheumatism and the widow in Caldwell.

The odor of the sizzling steaks was torment that made Stub weak. He moved the coffee pot when Cinches told him to, and the steamy vapors made his mouth water.

"That Curley is a knife man, huh?" Stub asked.

"Just a little crazier than the average trail hand," Cinches snorted. "Last time up he had a ruckus with a gambler. He figures he's going to slice that gambler into strips this time, and maybe clean out half the Yankees up North."

Stub had to move away from the cooking odors. He was loosening the latigo on Hilb when he saw Kinard, riding in. The trail boss swung down and watched Cinches pour cornmeal batter into a pan. Without looking at Stub, Kinard said: "I told you to beat it."

Cinches looked at the two men. "Oh," he muttered. "He's hungry, Kirby."

"Sure," Kinard said. "But he didn't get hungry working for me. He's been laying out on our flank like an Indian for two days and nights."

"I had my reasons," Stub said, "and they're none of your business. I still want that job, Kinard."

The trail boss looked at Stub without expression. "You can stay to eat. That's the last I want to see of you."

Someday I'll kill him! Stub thought. He walked over to Hilb and tightened the latigo. "Keep your stinking grub, Kinard. Shove it somewhere!" He swung up and rode away, his head held high.

Cinches stared after him and said something to Kinard, who shook his head.

Fury made twisted knots in Stub. He rode far to the west

of the drive and sat behind a hill. There were a lot of reasons why he didn't have to go with this herd. He could catch on with the next drive. But that might be weeks away. There was one big reason why he did have to work this drive: no sharp-nosed son-of-a-bitch with a hat like a gourd was going to tell him what he couldn't do.

Stub was going with the drive, and, afterward, he would kill Kirby Kinard, and maybe Curley Volland, too.

He paced the flank the rest of the day. His anger was tempered by the dry burning of hunger, but still his determination was an overriding force. He made his outcast camp that night, drinking water until his stomach rolled and bubbled with the burden.

Hilb's whickering roused him. Something was creeping in. Soft, regular thuds, rustling grass. Stub rolled out of his blankets and tried to see along the ground. The sounds came closer.

"Sing out, or I'll blast the belly off you!" he challenged.

"Kinard!"

The trail boss came on in. His horse was a great bulk against the sky. "What are you figgering on doing out here?"

"It's a free country."

"Answer some questions for me."

Stub was silent. Kinard's sharp manner was unchanged, but there was hope in his presence. "Where'd you get your horse and rig?"

"I got them from my family. I swiped them."

"Your old man was mean to you?"

"No." The quick answer surprised Stub. "I just got tired of him."

"Your brothers picked on you?"

"No. I could lick most of them."

"Why'd you leave home?"

"I got sick of taking orders."

"Yeah," Kinard said dryly. "What do you think you'll have to do if I hire you?"

"That's some different."

"Is it?" Kinard was bitter. "Let's find out."

"You're hiring me?"

"Come on."

They rode toward the camp together. Now that he was in, Stub changed his mind slightly about Kinard. He wouldn't have to kill the man, after all. The thought of food was overpowering.

"All right," Kinard said, "go over to the cavvy and let Jinglebob get some rest until morning."

"Without eating?"

"You heard me."

Stub hated him more than ever then. Kinard went on toward the fire. A few moments later Stub saw him standing there, drinking coffee. When Stub told Jinglebob he could go to bed, the kid said: "So you finally weaseled in."

"You looking for a mouthful of busted teeth?"

Jinglebob backed up. "*You* sure are."

111

So Wyatt Monroe went north with the first drive of the year. No one called him Nueces, they called him Stub, and he knew then that his father had talked to Kinard. He stood most of the night guard on the rounds. During the days he rode drag, eating the dust of old cows, the tired cows, and cows that had dropped calves on the march. Sometimes he got four hours of sleep a night. What other rest he got came at odd moments of driving in the saddle.

Kinard saw that he did more than his share of rustling for the cook. Stub accepted it. He grew gaunt and savage, but he was not going to let Kinard break him. He developed a fine hate for the men he worked with, but the job itself was not too big.

From Bull Foot he learned that the drive was a shoe-string gamble by Kinard, who had gathered a large part of the herd by cow hunting far to the west during the winter. Stub openly expressed the hope that Kinard would go belly-up on the deal, but yet Stub worked harder than any other man of the crew to keep the drive going.

Two days across the Colorado, Stub was drinking coffee at the fire just before going on night guard, when Curley came in from the herd. "I'll give you one last chance, Stub. My pistol and a P.H. knife for that Walker."

"Let's see the knife."

"I ain't never seen the Walker yet."

Curley's pistol was old Army. It would do. But Stub shook his head. "I ain't much interested in that damned relic you carry." He turned his back.

Curley dragged a blanket from a roll. He put his pistol and a green-handled clasp knife on it. "You started to trade, Stub. I don't like Indian givers." His eyes glittered as he looked at the sheen on the butt grips of the Walker.

Stub hesitated a few moments longer. "Straight across. No bellyaching afterward."

"Put it on the blanket," Curley said.

Bull Foot and Benje Sanders came in closer to see the trade. Cinches rolled out from under the wagon and hobbled over to the fire. The knot Stub cut low on his holster was one anchor end of a piece of rawhide that was twisted around the barrel of the Walker to keep it from leaving the holster, and for good reason. Lever and rammer and barrel halfway back to the frame were rusted into uselessness. Mike had found the pistol half buried in mud near one of the lakes at home, and he had pulled the same trick Stub was using now to get rid of the weapon.

Stub dropped the worthless pistol on the blanket and gathered up Curley's Colt and knife. Curley took one savage look at the Walker. He kicked it into the fire. "Fork over my stuff!"

"You traded." Stub was not quite ready for the blow Curley struck him in the face, but he acted quickly a second later. He butted Curley in the chin. They twisted across the blanket, windmilling, grunting. Stub's wrists and hands were mostly hard bone, and the top of his head was solid. He butted Curley in the face again, rushed him across the fire, tripped him, and fell on top of him. Then he pounded at Curley's face until Curley went limp.

Stub swaggered back to the blanket. He picked up the pistol and knife and put them away. He looked at the three men standing near the fire. One of them had laughed when he first saw the Walker, but now all three of them were silent, staring curiously at Stub. *Afraid of me,* Stub thought with a swift rush of pride. That was good.

"All right!" Curley was on one knee, with his knife poised over his shoulder. "Get out of the way, Cinches!"

The cook moved quickly.

It struck Stub with brutal impact; this was not home; this was not the Monroe give-and-take society, where a last play or a word out of turn meant no worse than a fist fight. He glanced at Bull Foot, who was the closest to being a friend. Bull Foot was not going to lift a hand. Sanders was looking away.

Curley rose. There was blood on his mouth and the ringlets of his beard glistened with blood. He came forward like a cat. "I'm going to learn you a thing or two about a knife, Stub. I'm going to carve you where you live."

Kinard's voice was bitterly cold. He walked out of the night until the firelight caught the sharp planes of his face. "Put the knife away, Curley." With his hands at his sides Kinard was twice as dangerous as Curley. Stub sensed it instantly.

Curley put the knife away. He picked up his hat. "You made the worst mistake of your life, Stub."

Kinard said: "Don't try to correct any mistakes during this drive, Curley. You made a damn' fool trade."

"Sure he did!" Stub laughed.

Kinard knocked him down with a cracking blow that came from nowhere. When Stub's shock wore into anger, he was on his haunches. He fully intended to rise and tromp Kinard into the ground, but the trail boss stood there, relaxed, watching him with such a thoughtfully mean expression that Stub knew true fear of another man for the first time in his life. Before Stub could make rage smother fear, Kinard walked into the night.

Stub overheard Cinches and Bull Foot talking about it afterward. Cinches said: "Ordinarily that would have been the funniest thing I ever seen, the look on Curley's face and all, but with Stub . . . it just ain't funny somehow."

"Funny as a grave," Bull Foot said. "That's where Stub is headed."

Curley became a spur, roweling persistently in the back of Stub's mind, but there was too much work to worry overly about him. There were the sleepy nights with the remuda, with Kinard drifting out of the blackness almost silently to make his checks. By day the clashing of broad-pointed horns, the rattling and clashing of hocks. Dust. Red-eyed, lean riders spitting dust, whacking with reatas, letting the herd follow its instincts, merely slapping and guiding the drive.

It was a good life, Stub decided. Action removed part of his discontent, but there was a different roiling in him now. The crew was barely civil to him, and Kinard not at all, and the to-hell-with-them line of his thinking did not fill an emptiness in his daily living.

Long striding steers on point made the pace misery for the slow and weak animals of the drag. The riders shot spindle-legged calves that lagged. Some of them Curley killed with his knife, spinning it into their throats, grinning at Stub afterward, making his promise and his threat. There was no easy dozing in the saddle now. Enraged cows tried to break back down the miles dotted with small blue and red carcasses, and it took constant alertness to beat them back into the drive.

Bull Foot was the only one whose temper did not strain wire-tight. He did his work and spoke of the pasture up North where the riding would be easy and town only a few miles away. But even he went over the edge just before the crossing of the Brazos.

They made fifteen hard miles to reach the river late one afternoon, coming in against a bend with the sun quartering behind them. There was only a hundred yards of swimming water. The cows were warm, and they went in readily enough, but on the far bank they began to spread and get out of hand, and then, as if by sheer perverseness, they found a long strip of floating sand and began to bog down.

The operation became a temper-cracking chore. When a cow was hauled free on the end of a reata, it tried to kill the rider who had saved it. While that was going on, more animals crowded in to bog themselves. It was almost dusk when the drivers cleared the riverbank. Someone had made a mistake, not scouting that bar of mush sand, Stub kept saying.

He was loud about it, for Kinard's benefit.

Kinard paid him no attention. The other riders merely gave him weary, disgusted looks, until Bull Foot at last told him savagely to shut up.

"Make me," Stub said.

"The world is full of men that can do it," Bull Foot said. "I'm one of them, too, but right now I got other things to do."

In straggles they pushed the herd up the bank to high bed ground not far from where Cinches was cooking supper. It was near the finish when a blue roan steer broke from a bunch Bull Foot and Stub were driving.

"Turn that bugger!" Bull Foot yelled.

Still rankling over Bull Foot's insult, Stub said—"Turn him yourself."—although he was closer to the steer than Bull Foot. And then, from habit, Stub went after the animal. . . . He started too late. The steer high-tailed toward the wagon. It would have gone on past, but Stub made another mistake, misjudging the distance he had to turn the steer. Instead of putting it back toward the herd, he bent it into the camp.

Cinches dived to the side of the wagon. The blue roan kicked the supper to kingdom come. Cinches made another pot of coffee and said that was it: if ten riders couldn't keep one cow out of the camp, they didn't deserve to eat. He crawled under the wagon and lay there with his rifle in his hands, daring anyone, including Kinard, to try to make him cook.

Curley cursed like a madman. He stopped suddenly, looking at Stub. "He done it."

The five riders who had come in to eat in the first shift were caked with dust and sweat, tired, hungry, their tempers on the surface. Curley went to the wagon and dragged out his *chaparejos*.

Steve Frazee

"No you don't!" Stub reached toward his pistol. Someone hit him across the knees from behind. He went down, and someone grabbed his pistol. Four more men took their *chaparejos* from the wagon. Kinard gave Stub a slow, calculating look and made no move to stop his crew.

Stub would not run. He tried to fight. There were five men around him. They tripped him. The heavy bull-hide chaps slashed him, wrapping around his neck and jerking him off his feet. The leather was heavy. Much of it was imperfectly tanned, and some of the chaps bore heavy conchos. Stub charged one way, and then another. There was always the buffeting of leather against his face, the pound of it on his back and shoulders. Curley held his chaps by the bottom and let the belt and the strap swing free.

The buckle smashed into Stub's mouth. His hands and wrists were bleeding. He made a desperate effort to get at Curley's sneering face. The stiff edges of someone's chaps caught him across the temple and felled him. He rose to his hands and knees.

They beat him down and kept whaling him after he was flat. Kinard said tonelessly: "Let him go."

Stub was hurt, but it was fury, rather than injuries, that kept him weak and almost helpless on the ground. With his head on one arm, spitting blood from his lips, he watched Kinard and the cowboys drinking coffee. They barely glanced at him.

They eyed him bleakly when he finally rose and staggered over to Kinard. "Where's my pistol, Kinard?"

"You want it now or tomorrow?" Kinard asked thinly.

"Now."

Kinard went to the wagon and got the pistol. He held it out, his eyes dark and steady. There was a sureness in him that gave Stub pause. He wanted to grab the weapon and empty it into the men standing at the fire, starting with Curley.

"Take it," Kinard said.

Slowly Stub reached out, half expecting trickery. He saw the caps on the nipples, the charges in place. There was a tense, singing moment when he held the weapon in his hand. Kinard watched him steadily. The red-eyed men at the fire were set like trap springs.

Stub slid the pistol into his holster.

"Night guard. Now," Kinard said. "Get out there." He turned his back and walked away, but it was still he, and not the watchful men at the fire, who kept Stub from drawing the pistol. For the first time Stub's fear of the trail boss was tinged with respect. But he still hated Kinard, he thought bitterly. When the drive was over, he would have to kill Kinard.

The bedded herd was restless. Cows that had lost calves kept milling uncertainly, and a few big steers, always veterans at communicating unrest, kept getting up and down. *I hope they break and scatter from hell to breakfast and he never finds them,* Stub thought. But still he kept riding slowly along his section of the herd, trying to sing through battered lips.

It was a black night. The fire at the wagon was a pleasant beacon. Someone from the other side of the herd had gone in for coffee and was squatted on the ground with a tin cup that caught the tinkle of the firelight. Across the Brazos, a few cows that had swum back after being hauled from the sand bawled mournfully for dead calves.

Kinard came from the darkness, riding slowly around the herd. "How are they, Stub?"

"All right," said Stub curtly.

"Keep 'em that way." Kinard paused. "Go in for coffee, if you want."

"I don't want any."

Steve Frazee

"Suit yourself." Kinard paused a moment longer, and then he rode away and Stub heard him talking to the next night guard.

Bastards, all of them! The thought did not help fan the anger Stub felt against the world; it left, instead, a lostness in him and a kind of loneliness he'd never felt before. But he repeated it again.

The deep rise of night came. Wild by heritage, the herd rose, sniffing the air, listening. Each animal seemed to turn, jostling, and then they took assurance from the quietness, from the plaintive crooning of the riders. The herd bedded down again, chewing, grunting. Bone-weary and discouraged, Stub hooked one leg around the horn and stared into the night.

Bull Foot came out. "Go get your beauty rest, Stub." He spoke as if nothing had happened.

"To hell with the camp."

"Suit yourself." Bull Foot was unconcerned, and it struck Stub that the beating he had taken was not a highlight in the lives of the men who had given it. It was like any part of the drive to them. It made him small in his own eyes. He tried hard to kindle rage, but he was too bodily sore and tired of mind.

He rode in and went to bed. In the morning the crew paid less attention to him than before. Except Curley. Curley spun his heavy knife and smiled. "One day closer to the end of the drive, Mister Stubborn. I'm looking forward to that a whole lot."

IV

They left the Trinity far behind. Rains caught them six days short of the Red. Only Cinches had a heavy outer garment, a

118

Confederate greatcoat that he wore as he slipped in the mud around his fire trench, cursing the sputtering rain.

Wet when they rode, wet when they slept, the drivers ate watery food for four days. A warm, steamy odor came from the herd, on the march and on each bed ground. Behind it, across the rolling hills, lay a muddy track a hundred yards wide. Kinard was ornery-sharp with everyone.

The rain ended one night. The next day, slowly warming after the start, the herd plodded across a steaming land under a vast blue sky. Golden eagles dipped low. The bones of long-dead cows began to dry once more, gleaming white in the green flush of spring.

Stub couldn't get enough of being alive. He wanted to sky-lark. He wanted to chat with Bull Foot, but there were burrs still sticking in his mind, so he put a sullen front on his mood. No one seemed to care.

They approached the Red on an afternoon when the clouds were cottony bursts all over the sky. Stub's first look at the river stunned him. He whispered: "My God!" He was staring across a half mile of surging power, the likes of which he had never dreamed of. He saw a cottonwood go by, spinning silt from its branches as it turned. It went under, and then the great spokes of its roots shot up, twisting in the tawny flood. An instant later the racing water dragged it out of sight. Sheets of foam as big as the porch at home were slapping in the middle of the river.

The opposite bank looked very far away. Stub felt an urge to test himself and his horse against the power, to rip through the current and plunge out triumphantly on the other side.

Kinard rode up beside him. "Makes a man damned small, don't it?"

"It's a beaut!" Stub said. "When do we hit it?"

"Right away. Sometimes it turns into a mess out there, if

the cows get to milling. If that happens, you stay clear, hear me?"

The rebel came up in Stub. "You think I'm not man enough to handle that kind of. . . ."

"Do as I say. Now get back to the herd and tell Bull Foot and Benje to come up here right away with Cinches and the wagon."

Stub did not see the wagon cross; he saw it afterward in the shallow water on the other side, its tongue unbolted and the water streaming from its bed. Kinard and Bull Foot were cutting loose cottonwood logs they had lashed to the running gear.

Kinard and Sanders came back across the river, towed along beside their mounts. The heads of the horses were only tiny spots in the flood. They landed a quarter of a mile downstream. Stub had changed to Hilb because Pa had always said the blue roan was a swimmer. Like most of the crew, Stub was stripped down to boots, underwear, and hat.

Kinard and Sanders came from downriver, dripping, still spitting silt. "Chouse 'em down the draw," Kinard said. "Keep 'em moving."

Stub watched the lead steers take the water, bending at the knees and going in with a lunge. The riders kept ramming them down the draw, forcing the pressure on the hesitant. Velocity shot the leaders downstream in an instant. They slanted with the power until they reached a still area near the far bank, and then the operation became a tremendous snake that fed its sections in on one bank, bent into a deep U where the violent current ran, and writhed out through shallow water where Bull Foot and three others kept the cattle moving toward a holding ground just above the river.

About two thirds of the herd was over before Kinard said: "Go ahead, Stub. Give Curley a chance to warm up."

His first hard contact with the water made Stub whoop. Then the current had him, and the steady, driving power of it made him afraid. He was too tense to look at Kinard on the upstream point, too chilled to do anything but pray for the far bank to come closer. Slapping water covered Hilb's head. Stub slid over his saddle and swam behind, holding to the flowing tail, riding high to keep from being kicked.

He was terrified until the flow of swimming cows bent upstream and sharp backs began to rise above the dirty water. He hauled himself back on Hilb then, and made a show of herding cattle that knew where they were headed better than he. He lost some of his terror on the re-crossing, but he knew that he finally found something to scare the blooming daylights out of him every time he bucked it.

Kinard seemed to think there was nothing unusual in a man's first crossing of the Red. Curley said: "Don't drown yourself, Stub. I'd be awful put out not to see you in Caldwell when the drive is over."

The trouble came when the weak ones of the drag were crossing. Stub didn't know what had started it, but all at once the deepest part of the U broke, and cows tried to swim in all directions. They reared on each other's backs, moaning. The Red was sweeping them away.

Kinard yelled: "Stay clear!" He himself went into the mill, striking with his quirt, trying to force a point toward land. Stub slapped his horse's head upstream and let the tangle drift down on him, in order to do what Kinard was doing.

They were both into it then, and Stub knew what a fool he was. Crushed against struggling longhorns, the horses could not kick to stay afloat. Kinard's mount went down first. Stub saw Kinard kick up from the saddle and grab the horn of a cow on the outer rim of the mill. He tried to turn the cow toward the north bank, but she went, instead, back into the current. And then she went down. Kinard beat the water clumsily, holding his head high.

Stub's horse was compressed in the mill. A cow that was crowded under fought to reach the surface. It drove a horn into Hilb's belly. Another cow tried to climb on the horse's back. Hilb screamed, and then the water had him. Stub used the last instant of his mount's floatage to launch himself in a belly flop across the neck of a steer. He grabbed the tossing horn of another longhorn and rode it down. Fighting for his life, he swam and crawled and kicked his way over the backs of drowning animals until he broke free.

The current had swept him along with Kinard, who was still pounding water, strangling now. Stub swam to him and got him by the hair. The south shore was only a hundred feet away, but after the first minute of swimming Stub knew he would never make it with Kinard, and probably not alone, either. He held to Kinard and kept trying to swim.

Curley had acted instantly, galloping along the bank, then plowing down and lifting his horse in a leap from crumbling dirt. He shouted wildly at Stub. His reata was ready, but Curley had to quarter into the current to make his throw reach. The leather skidded across Stub's shoulders. He went under when he quit swimming with his free hand to grab the rope, which slipped greasily through his fingers until the hondo gave him a grip.

Jinglebob made the final play. He shot a loop to Curley who put it on his horn, and then Jinglebob's horse quarter-faced the tug, and the current swung Curley and the other two against the shore.

Kinard coughed until his eyes were red, streaming pits. His lips were blue. "I told you to stay clear, Stub. But you're a fool, and there ain't no cure for you."

Hurt came before the anger this time: this was the thanks

you got for trying to save a man's life. Stub glanced at Curley and Jinglebob. Curley was coiling his reata, stripping the water from it with his fingers.

"There's a cure for him, sure enough," he said. "I got it."

"I'd have let *you* drown!" Stub said.

"You ain't me." Curley grinned. "No river is going to cheat me."

"Shut up, all of you!" Kinard said. "Get back to work."

They all crossed with the last bunch of cows. From then on Kinard was scarcely even civil to Stub, and Stub recalled something his father used to say. Doing a man a favor often made him hate you more than if you harmed him. Thinking of his father, Stub felt guilty about the loss of his saddle. And Hilb was gone, too, somewhere far downstream with two hundred cows that would drift into a shallows, so bloated that their long legs would look stubby.

As soon as the herd was bunched on their bed ground, Stub borrowed a saddle from Bull Foot and started downriver on a fresh horse. Kinard intercepted him. "Where do you think you're going?"

"To look for my blue roan. Maybe he drifted ashore, and I can get the saddle back." There were still two hours of daylight left.

"I got a saddle down there, too, but there ain't no time to look for it. Use an extra rig out of the wagon or ride bareback to Caldwell. Now get back to the remuda and let Jinglebob come in to eat."

"The hell with you, Kinard. I'm looking for my. . . ."

"No, you ain't!"

Kinard was five times meaner than Sant Monroe ever had been. Come to think of it, his father never had been mean. Stub tried to stare the trail boss down and lost the duel.

"When this drive is over, Kinard. . . ."

"Yeah, yeah, when the drive is over, you'll cut a fat hog in the hind end. Now get back to the remuda."

The score against Kinard was heavier than ever when Stub rode away to obey orders.

For several days before the drive reached Red Fork Ranch, there was a quickening of interest among the cowboys, more laughter and horseplay than Stub had seen before. He had no part in it. Too many people in the world were against him, and he had to settle with them.

At sundown one day they fought the herd into the funneling wing walls of the big log stockade at Red Fork. The corral held them all, nearly twenty-five hundred head.

After supper the crew went to the store to celebrate their one night's relief from the routine of the trail. They stuffed themselves on ginger snaps and canned peaches. Two red-bearded bullwhackers who were camped nearby took turns at playing the violin.

Kinard's drivers danced, an enthusiastic exhibition of stomping and jumping. Bull Foot worked up a full head of steam. The sweat gleamed on his round face as he grinned his bullfrog grin and emptied his pistol into the dirt floor. Curley whooped and hurled his knife into the ceiling joist, and then he leaped high to retrieve it.

Sitting alone on a box in the corner, Stub watched uncertainly. Even Cinches was kicking up. No one paid Stub any attention. They were all fools, he told himself, acting like kids because of this one-night break in the grinding life of the trail. He rose suddenly and left.

Lying in his blankets beside the corral logs, he heard the noise at the store go on and on. It created the feeling of loneliness in him, and he thought that if he could start up the trail again maybe he would act differently. He was a man, as he had claimed at home, but maybe his father had been right: he didn't act like a man in all things.

Late in the night he heard Kinard herding the crew back to their beds outside the corral. Cinches said: "What happened to Stub?"

"Who cares a damn?" Curley said. "I'm more interested right now in what happened to that second jug of whisky them bullwhackers had."

"I put it in safe keeping for them," Kinard said. "You can get your whisky at the end of the drive."

The group stumbled on in the inky darkness.

Curley was surly when he spoke again. "I think I'll find where Stub is sleeping and throw a bucket of water on his blankets."

"Go ahead," Bull Foot said, "but I don't advise it."

"Why not?"

"He might throw something back a damned sight harder than water. That Stub's like a rattler with a knot in his tail. He's likely to make a pass in any direction."

Caldwell and the end of the drive. Stub saw his first rails. Most of the town came down to the loading pens and holding grounds to see the first drive of the year, but still it did not seem to Stub that there was half the excitement in being here that he had anticipated.

All the other drivers were swaggering or in a festive mood. Cinches pointed out the boarding house owned by the widow. He pulled some clothes out of his war bag and beat the dust out of the garments on a corral pole. "When she says . . . 'Cinches, are you figuring to stay this time?' . . . I'll say . . . 'Honey Pot, you done got yourself a man for keeps'."

Benje Sanders asked Bull Foot where his little settling-down pasture was, and Bull Foot was vague. "Not right around here, I guess. Maybe a little farther west, or somewhere."

Curley came back from town mean drunk. He sunk his knife into a corral post and eyed Stub. Kinard said: "This drive ain't over until the herd is sold." He looked at Stub as if Stub were something that had just crawled out of the brush.

"I don't need your help, Kinard," Stub said. "Let him start something any old time. I got a thing or two to settle with you, too."

"In due time," Kinard said.

Kinard made his deal two days later. Stub was the last man to be paid off. The others had gone racing into town. Stub had more money in his pockets than he'd ever seen before. Kinard counted out the last coin and stepped back.

"Now, what's on your mind, Stub?"

"The way you treated me."

Kinard nodded. "Just how do you mean?"

"To start with, I was half starved and you refused to give me. . . ." Stub stopped. His complaint, he realized, was ludicrous. No one had asked him to run away from home, to lie out on the prairie and go hungry. All the time he had been sure that he had a terrible mass of grievances against Kinard, but when he tried to single them out one by one, the only beef that seemed real was the fact that Kinard had not let him go look for his saddle at the Red. But Kinard had not taken time to go look for his horse and saddle, either.

Stub was confused. The hard core of his resentment against Kinard came unstuck. He was supposed to hate the man, and he guessed he had, but now the reasons were no good. Still, he had made his threats, and here was Kinard waiting for him to carry them out.

"Go on, Stub."

"I promised to settle with you."

"So you did," Kinard said. "Before it starts, I want to know what for."

"Don't you try to smooth-talk me out of it!"

"I ain't. Make up your mind."

The quality that had given Stub his name told him he was obliged to make a fight, although he had no real wish to do so, and no solid peg on which to hang a reason. He watched Kinard's sharp face and saw all the marks of danger. A taunt or amusement in the man's expression would have been enough to tip the balance, but Kinard showed only a slight bitterness and patience that Stub had never noticed before.

"I haven't got anything against you," Kinard said.

Stub felt a great lessening of tension. There was an honorable way out of this, after all.

"Except," Kinard said deliberately, "you've got a chip on your shoulder as big as Texas. You're a knot-headed trouble-maker, just like your old man said."

It was so. Stub did not intend to admit it aloud, but it was true. It was the realization of that, rather than the wholesome fear he felt of Kinard, that made him say: "Well, maybe I ain't got anything against you, either." He was relieved and surprised to find that there was no weakness in the statement.

But his old resentments against anyone who gave him an order were still ready to flare. He studied Kinard narrowly, watching for a sneer, for any expression that would say Kinard thought he had no courage to fight.

Kinard's face was grave. "Your old man came out the first night you left home. He said you'd probably skulk along our flank for a day or two, trying to fool somebody, and he said it was all right with him if I hired you. He made you a present of that saddle the Red got. I like your old man, Stub. I'd say it would do you good to make an effort to be like him." Kinard spun around and mounted his horse. "Maybe you're learning." He turned and rode toward town.

After a time Stub saddled up and went in himself. He saw a lilac bush in a yard and reined over to have a closer look. A woman watering flowers from a sprinkling can straightened up and said harshly: "What do you want, cowboy?" Stub touched his hat and rode on. He let the horse drink from a half hogshead at the town pump in front of the Leland House, looking across the street at the saloons.

He felt lonely and unwanted, but this time he told himself that it was partly his own fault.

V

When he bought new boots and clothes and saw the old ones in a dirty pile on the floor, he knew why the woman had given him such short treatment. It would be great, he thought moodily, if the orneriness in him could be shed like the rags at his feet. In a barbershop he bathed in a tin tub that was shaped like a soup tureen, and then he had a shave and a haircut. The taste of the twenty-five-cent cigar he bought in a saloon was not quite what he had expected.

He was leaning against an awning post outside, making a pretense of smoking, when Jinglebob reeled past. The youth stopped and made a turn, rocking on his heels. "You're due any time, Stub. Curley's got a gambler that robbed him last year to take care of first, and then. . . ."

"Why didn't Curley take care of him last year?"

His eyes bright with liquor, Jinglebob gave Stub a vicious look. "Just because you ran a bluff on me. . . ."

"Go on, or I'll finish it."

There was no pleasure this time in seeing the sullen fear in

Jinglebob's eyes. Stub watched him stagger into the Palace, wearing the same black-and-white-checked pants and run-over boots he had worn up the trail. The first time he saw Jinglebob, driving the remuda in the dust far below the Colorado, Stub knew he probably could have made a friend of him. It was too late now. Stub thought of several things that ran clear back to his quarrels at home. He had learned a lot on the trail up. He even allowed that some of it might have been knocked into him the hard way. But nothing he had learned would get him around Curley easily now.

Curley wasn't Kinard. Curley didn't give a damn what happened to Stub Monroe. Maybe Kinard didn't, either. Perhaps he was so disgusted with a knot-headed trouble-maker that he wouldn't care to say hello from now on.

All the way up the trail, almost drowned, and I didn't make one single friend, Stub thought. On top of that he'd made an enemy who was going to try to stick a knife into him like he'd killed those weak-legged calves.

Stub lounged against the post with a dead cigar clamped between his teeth and thought about his troubles until he built a terrible anger against Curley; and with it came a measure of the old, full-sweeping revolt against the world in general.

Kinard came out of the Leland House with a cattle buyer. The two men angled across the street. Kinard hesitated an instant, and then he said to the man: "See you inside in a minute, Liggett." He walked on up the street to Stub.

"You're waiting for Curley, huh?" Kinard asked.

"No. I'm going in after him."

"You'll kill him, say. Then you'll be all man, a regular heller who's made the trail and shot a man down."

"What else can I do?" Stub asked savagely.

"You brought it on," Kinard said. "Settle it your way."

Not one friend. To hell with them, Stub thought. *I don't need friends.* But he watched Kinard walk into the Palace and felt a loss. What did Kinard expect him to do? Run away, or go in and give Curley his pistol back and try to apologize?

Stub was still biting on the cigar when he walked into the Palace a few minutes later. He saw Bull Foot and Sanders and three others of the crew that had come up the trail with him. Kinard and the cattle buyer were sitting at a table. Jinglebob slid through a doorway in the back of the room. A few moments later Curley stepped out. The knife was in the case at the back of his left shoulder, and he was wearing, also, a pistol he had bought from Benje Sanders. *Habit would make him try the knife first and the pistol second,* Stub thought.

Curley's teeth and the whites of his eyes gleamed against his dark beard as he walked forward.

"That's far enough," Stub said. He had to keep Curley as far away as possible and then follow out his own plan to the letter. But already his side just above his left hip was cold, and he could not forget how some of the calves had died below the Brazos.

Stub saw only movement and no detail. He turned sidewise and put his fist hard against his chin, shielding his throat with his bent wrist, holding the rest of his arm tightly against his body. The knife was only a blur. It ripped the front of Stub's stiff new shirt and was gone.

Stub had his pistol clear a second later. The hardest part of the whole affair was not to kill Curley then. In spite of himself, Stub started to press the trigger. He fought against the urge a second time when, in desperation and too late, Curley put his hand on his own pistol.

"Hold it!" Stub said. He saw Curley's hands drift out to the sides, palms down. The man's forehand and cheek bones were a dirty gray color. He stood stiffly, staring, a man waiting for the smash of lead.

Curley was not worth killing. Stub had his triumph over him now, but he had a greater one, a victory over himself. He realized it. He wished he could spare a glance to see how Kinard was taking it.

"Get his pistol, Bull Foot," Stub said sharply.

Peering around the end of the bar where he was crouched, Bull Foot said: "It ain't mine."

Stub walked forward. All the way he was afraid that Curley would still try for his pistol. Then he was close and the fear was gone. He dropped his own weapon and hit Curley in the same motion. In a twisting, savage scuffle he got the man's half-drawn six-shooter and threw it to one side.

He hammered Curley down and helped him up, and beat him down again. When at last Curley lay motionless, no one had to drag Stub away from him.

Stub turned to Kinard. "That's the way you wanted it done, huh?"

"Not me. It was your affair, Stub. You don't like anyone to tell you what to do."

Stub looked at the men he had come up the trail with. They eyed him quietly, neither afraid of him nor suddenly overly friendly. Only Jinglebob was greatly concerned; he sneaked out the back door.

A bartender threw a bucketful of water on Curley, who revived only partially. A bouncer then dragged him into the corner, out of the way.

Men went back to the bar. Conversations lifted once more. No one in the Palace gave a hang about what Stub Monroe had done. The realization helped put certain facts into focus for him. The world was not watching his every move, and the world was some larger than the chip he had for such a long time been carrying around on his shoulder.

He picked up his pistol and his hat and went toward the door, going a step out of his way to kick Curley's knife under a table.

He stood for a while by the awning post where he had been a few minutes before when it seemed most important that he kill Curley. It scared him to think how dangerous he had been then, for he had hated not only Curley but just about everyone in the form of man. No matter if he had to tangle with Curley again, he had licked himself at last.

The idea had been his own, when it finally came about, but no matter what Kinard said, it was still he who had suggested it indirectly. The poison of senseless rebellion was out of Stub's mind now, but still he did not have a friend.

Lonelier than ever, he went slowly down the street.

VI

Stub ate that night in the boarding house and paid for a room in advance. Cinches's widow was as lean as a roadrunner. Her hair was gathered in a hard knot at the back of her head, and she moved with a jerky briskness. The food she served was good.

Cinches came from the kitchen all aglow, clean-shaved, wearing new clothes and a white apron. When the widow understood the two men had been trail mates, her manner toward Stub was at once forbidding.

"I hear the boys are headed back tomorrow," Cinches said. "Not me, though. I'm glad I saw the light."

So Kinard was going back to Texas. No one had said anything to Stub about it. They didn't want him. He was not humble enough to accept the thought without anger, but there was no longer the perverse pleasure he had once felt in being an outcast.

Stub went to bed early. At dawn he was at the livery stable. The little grulla he had been using and the rig belonged to Kinard, who had sold the wagon and most of the remuda when he sold the herd. It was two hours before the drivers showed up. Jinglebob would not meet Stub's eyes, but the rest of the crew was not unfriendly.

"Where's Curley?" Stub asked Bull Foot.

Bull Foot blinked. "Don't you know? He got into it with that gambler he's been after and got himself plumb killed. We buried him this morning. That's why we're late."

They were talking the fact as they took a day's work on the trail. Stub made no comment.

"Where's Kinard?" he asked.

"He'll be along, I reckon, somewhere between here and Red Fork Ranch." Bull Foot swung up.

"I thought you had a little pasture where . . . ," Stub said.

"Don't pay no attention to what I say." Bull Foot grinned. He looked toward Texas. "So long, Stub."

They were not out of sight when Cinches came across the street, trying to hurry his toed-in, shuffling walk, glancing back across his shoulder. "Get my horse and get it quick!" he told the hostler.

Stub said: "I thought. . . ."

"Never mind what both of us thought! Some men just ain't constituted for settling down. I'll be driving a wagon on that trail until she's down ten foot deep in the ground and there's bridges across the Red."

Then Cinches was gone, making dust south. Stub watched him until he was out of sight.

The hostler grunted and disappeared into the stable. Down at the holding pens men were prodding cattle into cars.

Stub figured maybe he could get a job down there, but he kept looking south, thinking of the trail.

He had been a part of it, if but briefly. He knew what it took and what it gave, and he could thank it for helping straightening him out.

"Well, Stub?"

Stub turned to face Kinard. There was no use to ask Kinard anything. The man knew why he was here and what he wanted.

Kinard cocked his cigar and studied Stub with insolent gray eyes. "Think there's time to bring another herd up before snow flies, Stub?"

"Maybe."

"There's a drive that'll be gathered and ready against the time a man rides down to where it is." Kinard turned into the stable. "Somebody's got to ride that grulla back. Come on." Kinard grinned over his shoulder, and Stub saw a warmth in the man he had never understood before.

They rode away a few minutes later, cutting south through the most beautiful morning that the Kansas country had ever known.

McCorkhill's Private War

The Dutchmen started it. Their band slopped downhill through the clay until, a short distance from the Union outposts along the Rappahannock, the musicians fell into a loose formation and began to play "Morgenroth."

Private Gubby McCorkhill, of the 88th New York, the Irish Brigade, sat on a hacked stump near his hut and nursed the last of his tobacco by taking slow puffs on his stubby pipe. The first sergeant, Patrick Moylan, was fond of saying that "Morgenroth" was a stirring soldier tune—considering it was foreign. The only feeling the music stirred in Private McCorkhill was an increased desire to get his big red hands around the neck of a certain Rebel picket across the river.

For one of the few times since Fredericksburg there was no sleet. The ragged men in blue were not all crouched inside their huts this evening as the Southern dusk came down with a golden softness. Across the stream the Rebels were plain to see, eight thousand of them, and here the same number of fighting men. Two armies waiting on the winter.

At the moment only one enemy interested McCorkhill.

The music brought a second band of Dutchmen, and then a third and fourth came sloshing through the mud. They played "Bingen on the Rhine," and then they laughed at

135

themselves by playing "I Goes to Fight Mit Sigel." A roar of laughter went up on the darkening hillside.

On the Confederate shore a picket cried in a high, clear voice: "Play something real! Play 'Dixie'!"

Up where the 7th Wisconsin lived in huts of fence rails, mud, and canvas, a band struck up "Happy Land of Canaan." The musicians of a New Hampshire regiment came in. The Dutchmen went along. Now the occasional musket winks of pickets down the river were all stopped. The bands of two wild, Western regiments tramped up to join the Dutchmen.

There was a deep-voiced sigh when the last piece was done. Somewhere in the hastening gloom a colonel was bellowing for his musicians to assemble.

Where Southern campfires dotted the night, a band struck up "The Bonnie Blue Flag." The Johnny Rebs gave up a mighty cheer, and then the Union men yelled with them. One by one, like sparks igniting, a dozen bands on the Confederate side began to play the old Jacobite melody.

McCorkhill heard a Dutch bandmaster shout: "With them, with them! Now, blay!" Moments later the massed bands of both sides were joined.

Private McCorkhill began to tap his foot, and then he caught himself puffing his pipe to the rhythm of the music. He stopped both extravagances quickly, glowering toward the Rebel encampment.

When the last notes of "The Bonnie Blue Flag" died into the gloom, the same high-voiced Rebel picket shouted again: "Don't you Yanks know 'Dixie'?"

"Yah! For him now 'Dixie' we blay," the German leader said.

The Rebel picket who had yelled was not the one McCorkhill wanted to mangle. His man had a rough, deep voice, full of Irish mockery and insult. To think, an Irishman over there with heathen who yelled like banshees when they charged! It was, indeed, a sad commentary on the state of the Union. No doubt he was a renegade Irishman of some sort, possibly from an outlandish place like Sligo. Certainly not from Cork.

The last notes of "Dixie" were still alive when the Southerners swung out with "Maryland, My Maryland." *Ah! A true Rebel trick,* McCorkhill thought, catching the Union musicians with their breath still in their instruments. But his mind began to wander and his spine began to tingle. The air, such as it was, had certain good points. He put his left foot on top of his right brogan to keep the right foot still, and then he was short a foot to keep the left from tapping.

When the fiery note of "Maryland" drifted away, a distant Union band began the slow, sad music of "Tenting Tonight." Out of the night it grew in the voices of the soldiers, thousands of them standing in mud that was born when war was born.

They poured their souls into music that was at once a song of loneliness and a forgetting of the mud and sleet, the wormy hardtack, and the sickly blue beef, the Virginia quick-step, and the sons and brothers and comrades who could not rise at reveille. On the other side of the Rappahannock the ragamuffin army was singing, too. And it was over there that a band struck up "Home, Sweet Home."

One hundred and sixty thousand men tried to sing, but the song brought up remembered things that choked the effort. Softly, on both sides of the water, the bands went on alone. They finished, and then there was nothing left to play.

McCorkhill heard the Dutchmen slogging back to their miserable huts, and among them a drummer boy was sobbing. "Dot's all right now, Maxie," a thick German voice said. "Dot's all right."

A fine Rebel trick, indeed, making children cry like that, Private McCorkhill thought indignantly.

Sergeant Moylan was then beside the stump. "And what were you blubbering about, McCorkhill?"

"Hah! Blubbering, you say, Patrick Moylan. Go boil your shirt!"

"Blubbering just the same it is, all over the ugly hairy face of you. I've eyes for the dark."

"If there was a bit of moisture beside my nose, it came from peering so hard against the dark to see where that redhaired, bog-trotting. . . ."

"Him again," Sergeant Moylan said. "As I've told you before, McCorkhill, we've quiet on the picket line these days. Don't be thinking of disturbing a good thing. We've a gentleman's agreement with them across from us, the Mississippi Volunteers, in spite of Captain Marsh and his ideas of perpetual war."

"The Mississippi Volunteers, indeed!" Private McCorkhill tamped the ashes of his pipe hard to save the little tobacco that was left. " 'Twas them that shot our fine engineers off the spontoons at Fredericksburg, and then, after our artillery tumbled the town about their unwashed necks, they lay like cowards amongst the ruins and still kept shooting our engineers."

"The word you wish is *pon*-toons," Sergeant Moylan said loftily. "But be that as it may, we have a gentleman's agreement in our section. No shooting amongst pickets unless an officer is poking about, and no honest shooting even then. So mind your manners, no matter who you see across the water."

"Aw, go boil your shirt."

"Small wonder he made you gnash away at your rifle

under the hill that day, when all you could do was repeat low wit such as boiling my shirt." Sergeant Moylan started away, a big man who made heavy sounds in the mud. "Mind what I say now about keeping the peace whilst on picket duty."

"Aw, go. . . ." McCorkhill lapsed into moody silence.

A fine evening it had been, what with the music and then Moylan near ruining Private McCorkhill's dreams of revenge on a loud-mouthed, red-headed Confederate ape who had in truth made Gubby McCorkhill bite his rifle stock in terrible anger.

Out on the plain from looted Fredericksburg, that's where it was, there close to the sunken road at the foot of Marye's Hill. Even the Irish Brigade could not get to the stone wall at the foot of the hill. The height was a-smoke, and every whiff of the smoke carried a bullet or a charge of canister. In the sunken road behind the stone wall, which was as high as the belt of a tall cavalryman, the Rebel riflemen stood four deep, shooting as cool as you please.

There was a bit of a rail fence just ahead of a dip in the ground where all previous charges had broken. A handful of the 88th New York, leaning against the storm of lead, tramped on past the prostrate men in blue who tugged at their pants legs and said it was no use. A few of the handful reached the rails, not far from the long line of flame that kept running along the stone wall.

It was as far as anyone except Mead's Pennsylvanians got up the hill that day.

All at once Private McCorkhill knew he was alone. He was as flat as he could be behind a few rails with splinters sticking in all directions. Everything was smoke and noise. As far as he was concerned, all of Robert Lee's army was right there behind the stone wall.

Where now was the jaunty green banner the 28th Massachusetts had carried in the lead?

Private McCorkhill rolled on his back. He loaded his rifle and fired into the smoke toward the stone wall. The gush of fire betrayed him. Instantly some of the rocks tumbled from the rails, and splinters flew around his ears. After that he was content to lie still.

Just by cocking one eye he could see high up the hill where the gunners looked like fiends from hell around their pieces. Everything from up there went whizzing out on the plain where the long lines of blue kept coming up all day, never getting over the crest of the slight depression which, for all of Private McCorkhill, was now a million miles behind him. Dusk. The bullets from the prostrate men at the rear went over McCorkhill and spattered harmlessly on the stones of the wall in front of him. He tried to dig his chin into the ground.

Night. There was a thinning down of the firing then, but not enough. Bellies to the ground, the Union men behind McCorkhill kept shooting at the stone wall. A thousand tons of lead, he thought, and not one dead Rebel, and him trapped here on the frozen ground.

When the chill mists of morning were thick, the firing almost died away, and it was then McCorkhill heard them talking behind the stone wall. Cobb's Georgians. They bragged about it in a fearful language that was near foreign. But there was one voice that was clear enough, a rough, jeering Irish voice.

"I've a notion," it said, "to go out and pick up that pretty green banner with the harp upon it. It would make me a fine sash."

Somebody drawled, "They didn't leave it."

"They left everything else."

The Georgians laughed.

McCorkhill raised his head. He would get the green banner, would the lout! The traitorous, sneaking, behind-the-wall, flannel-mouthed. . . .

"Ah, well," the voice went on, "I'll have that pretty bit of cloth when it's light, after we've driven the whole shanty works of them into the river and are busy drowning them with long sticks."

"The way they came at us, they might take a heap of drowning," somebody drawled.

"Drunk, the pack of them! Our fine shooting sobered them up, and then they skedaddled. There's not an Irishman in all New York who can fight anybody but his wife. Now if *we* had been coming to take this road. . . ."

"Come out of your filthy trench and fight!" Private McCorkhill yelled.

There was a sudden silence behind the stone wall. Then the insulting voice said: "Now what was that mewing out in the fog, boys?"

"Me! Gubby McCorkhill of the Eighty-Eighth New York, the Irish Brigade, and damnation to you, you renegade Rebel scum!"

"Gubby. Gubby! Did you ever catch your foot in a hole, Gubby McCorkhill, that you couldn't skip back to the river with the rest of the cowardly Eighty-Eighth?"

"We'll be back!"

"You'll have to come by yourself, McCorkhill. The rest of the Irish Brigade died a-running."

The Georgians laughed again.

McCorkhill dug his fingers into the frozen clay. He was of a mind to charge through the mist and get his hands on the owner of the mocking voice. Then he could die happy. He raised up.

"Go boil your shirt!" he yelled.

* * * * *

The Irishman behind the wall dropped his voice, as if his words were for the Rebels only, but he spoke quite loud at that. "He's by the fence rails, boys. I remember him now, the big hairy-faced baboon who was lost in the smoke and trying to run back to the river. I seen he was mixed up, and out of the generosity of my heart I did not shoot his left eye out before his legs gave way from fright."

"You lie!" McCorkhill yelled. "Go boil your shirt!"

"You see, his mind is gone, and that is the only pleasantry he can shout. Come in, McCorkhill, and we'll help you over the wall, and maybe we'll pardon you for fighting on the side of foreigners and heathen."

McCorkhill inched his rifle above the barricade and snapped the hammer. The rifle had been neither capped nor charged.

"I can hear him grinding his teeth, boys. I swear it."

Beset by the most terrible, frustrating rage mortal man ever had to bear, McCorkhill was, in fact, biting at the forestock of his rifle.

From behind him, Sergeant Moylan called: "McCorkhill, you fool, come back here!"

"There's two of them alive!" the voice behind the wall said. "Who would have believed it?"

McCorkhill began to load his rifle. From the sound of the voice, his enemy was sticking his head above the stones. Keep him talking, keep him located, and then Private McCorkhill would blow his filthy voice right through the back of his neck.

"Have you got a name?" McCorkhill asked.

"I have."

"What is it?"

"General Jackson!"

McCorkhill was having trouble finding the cap box he had

taken off last night to give him a better fit against the ground. The laughter in the sunken road did not help.

"Crawl back here!" Moylan said.

"We'll be helping him do so," the voice announced. There were whispers behind the wall. "Now, boys, you know where he is. The first fifty on both sides of me. Ready!"

McCorkhill found the cap box.

"Aim!"

McCorkhill heard the click of heavy hammers. It sounded as though the whole of Lee's army was training on him. He dropped both cap box and rifle. He made a streak through the clay until he fell on top of a Union soldier, who cursed.

"Fire!" the voice cried.

"Boom!" the Rebels yelled, and then they began to shout derisively and laugh fit to kill.

"McCorkhill!" the voice called. "McCorkhill, where are you? I do believe he left us, boys. I'll miss his pleasant wit."

All Private McCorkhill could think to say was: "Go boil your shirt!" But he was too choked up to say even that.

McCorkhill heard afterward that Fredericksburg was a great battle, but the most he could remember was the taunting voice that had made him try to eat wood. Just two days ago, from across the Rappahannock, he had heard the same voice shouting insults at Federal pickets. And then he had seen the big, ragged Rebel standing easy over there, with a monstrous grin on his ugly face, with red hair sticking out all around the floppy brim of an old felt hat. It was enough to make an abolitionist out of an honest man.

Private McCorkhill rose from the stump. He went back to the hut where he lived with seven others.

Already in his bunk, Sergeant Moylan gave him a dubious eye. "Picket duty with Sergeant Lamb's detail for you to-morrow, McCorkhill."

"Indeed." McCorkhill removed his shoes and got into his bunk.

"It will be a fine, peaceful day, McCorkhill."

"Indeed." What a hell of a war!

All night McCorkhill suffered agonies. Again and again he had the red-headed Rebel lashed across the muzzle of a cannon, double-charged and double-shotted, with McCorkhill holding the lanyard and saying all manner of witty things. But something always happened. Before McCorkhill knew it, the Rebel was free and mocking him, and McCorkhill was grinding his teeth.

The morning was cold and misty. The coffee was weak, and the salt-side was extra stale. Private McCorkhill went on picket duty grumbling deep in his soul about the way the war was being run. Eight thousand men across the river and he could not shoot even the one that should never have been born!

Sergeant Lamb scrooched down in a nest of leaves that had been kept warm by the sergeant before him. He warned the detail to keep a sharp eye out for Captain Marsh, then went to sleep.

After a time the mists slid away, the sun came up, and in some ways it was a fine day. McCorkhill left his rifle in the limb of a tree and went down to the river where some of the 7th Michigan were playing with little boats.

Nobody had any tobacco to spare, but a wiry little corporal with no front teeth said: "Stick around, McCorkhill. We'll have plenty for all when we get the boats to working."

McCorkhill sat down beside a tall private of a Maine regiment, who was lounging on the bank, chewing tobacco.

"How about a bit of that for my pipe?" McCorkhill asked.

The Maine private spat. "Uhn-uh."

McCorkhill thought darkly that someday the Union might have to go to war with New England, also.

Under the Michigan corporal's direction, the soldiers launched three boats, with sails made from old shirts, with cargoes of coffee. Across the river a group of Rebel pickets lounged under the trees, waiting. The boats did well for about two hundred feet. Then they flopped over and went drifting down the river with their masts dragging.

One of the Confederate pickets yelled: "You Yanks don't know nothing!"

"Come over and launch 'em yourself, if you don't like it!" the corporal said. He sent out another craft laden with coffee. It capsized and drifted against a tangle of brush on a mud bar in the middle of the stream. "The wind's against us . . . or something!" He scowled at the man beside McCorkhill. "Johnson. You come from a sailing place. What's the matter with these boats?"

Johnson considered. "Sails ain't set right."

"Why didn't you say something before we lost four boats?"

Johnson considered again. "Nobody ast me," he said.

The soldiers laughed.

When Johnson set the sails, the boats went into the wind, made headway upstream, and beached nicely on the Rebel shore. Before long they came back laden with tobacco and Richmond newspapers. McCorkhill sliced plug into his pipe and lit up. It was not such a bad war, after all.

A moment later he almost bit his pipe stem in two. From across the river a great voice called: "Send us a Yankee newspaper, boys! We want to be amused by old Abe's lies."

There was the red-headed, bog-trotting. . . . McCorkhill did bite the stem of his pipe in two. His mind fell into an old trap. He bellowed: "Go boil your shirt!"

145

"McCorkhill! 'Tis himself, I swear. I thought you'd run clear back to New York by now, McCorkhill. Gubby, me boy, come over and maybe you can tell us who won at Marye's Hill."

"You know him, McCorkhill?" the corporal asked.

McCorkhill's reply was a groan.

"Boom!" the Rebel shouted. "And there went McCorkhill, running for the river!" He laughed like the great baboon he was.

"What's he talking about?" the corporal asked.

"Lies!" McCorkhill yelled. "Filthy lies! I'll crush him with my bare hands!"

Private Johnson squinted across the river. "It's a long way to reach."

The laughter astonished Johnson as much as it enraged McCorkhill. "Let me at him!" he howled.

Sergeant Lamb said: "Help yourself, McCorkhill . . . if you can swim like a mermaiden."

McCorkhill took off his shirt. He removed his shoes, and, since they were sound, he put them strictly into the keeping of Sergeant Lamb. "Come out of your trench and fight!" he yelled. "Come out, you. . . ."

"Your mind is gone again, McCorkhill! It's no trench but good Southern ground I'm standing on, where the miserable Eighty-Eighth will never set foot again."

McCorkhill started into the river. Sergeant Moylan came from the trees and grabbed his arm. "Now wait a bit!"

"Wait nothing. I'm going to bash his thick head in with his own musket!"

Moylan yelled across the stream. "The champion of the Eighty-Eighth New York, which is composed entirely of champion fighters, is coming to the island. Ten pounds of coffee against the same of tobacco he can beat your big-mouthed redhead!"

146

The maddest man in the Army of the Potomac tore away from Sergeant Moylan and plunged into the water.

"Twenty pounds of tobacco!" a Rebel picket shouted.

The cry—"Big thing!"—ran down the Yankee side of Rappahannock.

"No shooting!" Moylan yelled.

"No shooting!" the Rebels yelled.

McCorkhill paddled furiously. He saw a redhead bobbing strongly toward the island from the opposite bank.

"Get there first, McCorkhill!" Moylan shouted.

McCorkhill swam his best, but he could not do it. The other man was ahead of him, wading knee-deep in the glittering mud, a tremendous, grinning ape of a thing with great ears sticking out from the sides of his plastered hair. He was fully as hideous as McCorkhill had expected.

"You're as slow at swimming as you are with your wit." The man plucked a branch from the mud and used it to shove McCorkhill's head under water. He let McCorkhill come up and said: "Boil your shirt, McCorkhill, champion of the Eighty-Eighth New York, which is supposed to be a regiment."

McCorkhill sputtered and tried to get ashore. The island was a shifting, uncertain mess of silt. The Rebel pushed him under again, laughing. "I told you I would drown you with a long stick."

He let McCorkhill touch the island and let him scramble to his hands and knees. And then a mud-plastered foot as large as a slab of bacon kicked McCorkhill back into the river.

" 'Tis clumsy you are, Gubby McCorkhill of the Eighty-Eighth. Must I wait all day to break your puny ribs? Come on, man, come on, and stop floundering like some ugly water creature."

"I'm coming," McCorkhill growled. "Don't run away."

"Now, I wouldn't think of that." The Rebel laughed and kicked McCorkhill back into the water.

"I'm coming," McCorkhill said. This time the Rebel backed away and let him get ashore and gain his feet.

"A weak-looking thing you are, McCorkhill, to be challenging a man like Michael Finnessey."

McCorkhill lowered his head and plowed in. The mud was terrible. Big stars were exploding all over the place. Resting for a moment on his back in the silt, he heard Finnessey say: "Send over another Yankee!"

With an outraged grunt McCorkhill kicked Finnessey's legs from under him, then bounced up with as much bounce as he could manage, considering the island was nothing but thin lobscouse. He sprang like a tiger.

"So you're the dirty fighter, then," Finnessey said from where he was wallowing on his back like a stranded fish. He doubled his legs back. Both of his large feet caught Private McCorkhill in the face, fair in the midst of his tiger leap.

McCorkhill went into the mud with a sodden *thump,* believing for sure that his neck was broken. He heard Finnessey say, as if from a great distance: "I'm afraid you're ignorant of the rules of civilized warfare, Private McCorkhill."

Finnessey rose, putting a foot on the back of McCorkhill's neck and pushed his face into the silt. "Send over the whole regiment now! The specimen is giving me no exercise at all."

McCorkhill twisted about until he got a good grip on Finnessey's legs. He brought Finnessey down like a sack of frozen potatoes falling from a sutler's wagon. After a few minutes of gouging and battering, during which time McCorkhill tried to push several handfuls of mud down Finnessey's throat while Finnessey was doing his best to bite McCorkhill's hand, they both got to their feet.

"Your underwear," Finnessey said, panting, "is cleaner than when we started."

"Boil your shirt," McCorkhill said, and made a mighty swing, with the silt spinning from his arm all the way.

"Umm!" Finnessey said when the blow landed and the mud flew from his chin. He hit McCorkhill a resounding blow in the short ribs.

"Umm!" McCorkhill said, and struck Finnessey fair on his ugly nose.

"So it's a fair fight you're after?" Finnessey inquired.

They wallowed into each other, pounding away as if they were settling the war itself. After some time, when his body was all afire and his arms as heavy as the mud, McCorkhill decided that Finnessey must have his legs jammed into something, because he would not fall.

"What holds you up, Finnessey?"

"The great spirit of me."

McCorkhill hit him again. Finnessey hit him back. And that was about the last, for Finnessey started to go. By then McCorkhill was going, too. He managed to land on top, and the two of them slid part way into the river.

"Ah, now!" McCorkhill said, and pushed Finnessey's head under.

After a bit he let Finnessey come up for air, and to hear his last remarks. Finnessey blew hard, and then he grinned. "You lost your temper, McCorkhill. You. . . ."

"I did." McCorkhill shoved him under again. The next time he let him go, most of the mud was gone from Finnessey's face.

Finnessey sputtered and gasped, but he grinned once more. "To think you'd get mad," he said.

He had a fair grin, at that, and a good, clear Irish eye, such parts as McCorkhill could see beyond the swelling. It struck

McCorkhill that Finnessey had never been mad. He had been taunting and fighting on general principle.

Somewhat absently McCorkhill ducked him again.

Sergeant Moylan bellowed: "You idiot, McCorkhill, don't be drowning the man!"

McCorkhill pulled Finnessey out of the water and hauled him ashore. They sat in the mud like wounded turtles.

Sergeant Moylan yelled: "We win! Send the loot across. And since we have nothing better to do with our coffee, we'll send it over just the same."

The little boats plied back and forth.

"You're a powerful fighter," Finnessey said.

"You, too, Michael Finnessey. Where are you from?"

"Cork, and now New Orleans. It's a shame we wear different uniforms."

"It is," McCorkhill said. He struggled vainly with a sadness that he could not put into words.

After a time they staggered up.

"It's a weary man I am," Finnessey said. He put out his hand. They stood there with their muddy paws hard-gripped. Men on both banks cheered.

"And now it's the champion of the Seventeenth Regiment of Mississippi Volunteers you are, McCorkhill, as well as of the gallant Eighty-Eighth New York."

"I thought it was Cobb's men at the stone wall."

"Them and others and me of the Seventeenth that was run from the town. The green banner with the harp that shone so beautifully in the foul smoke,"—Finnessey blinked—"it's all right?"

McCorkhill nodded. He was blinking, too.

"I've got a drop of the river yet in my eye," Finnessey said. "When the bands played, the mist caused the same thing."

"I know," McCorkhill said. "You could go with me."

"And you could swim with me, also, McCorkhill."

They gripped their hands still tighter, considering problems beyond them, and then they walked to opposite sides of the mud bar.

"Don't be getting yourself killed, McCorkhill. On ground where my fine footwork will not be hampered, I'll be after regaining the championship someday by mashing your frightful face."

Some cold intuition told McCorkhill there would never be another meeting, but he grinned and said: "Sure, Mike Finnessey. Go boil your shirt."

They started then the lonely swim back to their respective shores.

Legacy of Violence

1

They saw the Sapinero six miles before the town of Kebler.
The cold current shouldered the horses downstream to a
poor landing in the willows, but Roderick Vail did not try to
seek a better course. He crashed his tall buckskin straight
through the growth, cursing when his horse stumbled in a
tangle of bone-gray débris left from flood time. He sent the
buckskin digging hard up the steep north bank. His mind
was set on something, and, when he was like that, he
slammed headlong into any barrier that seemed to block his
way.

Lee Vail, his son, came on more carefully, but when his
horse kicked the willows behind it, there was no choice about
the hill. The bay was heaving when it reached the mesa where
Roderick waited impatiently.

"That thing has got no guts," Roderick said. He was a
high-shouldered man, broad across the back, lean
throughout. Wet to the waist from the crossing, he took his
pistol belt from around his neck and strapped it on. He
checked the pistol. His hair was tawny, crisp, going down in
curling stair steps at the back. His eyes were cold blue. With
tapering, powerful fingers he plucked a piece of broken
willow from his hatband. "No guts at all," he said, looking at

his son's horse. The comment seemed to spread bitterly to cover other things.

Lee raised one leg at a time to let the water run from his boots. "There's a ford a half mile upstream."

"I rode this river when you were a snot-nosed kid." Roderick gave his son a weighing look, an expression charged with a thin stream of doubt.

These moments of sizing up had come more frequently of late. Lee had seen him look at his wife like that, mauling something in his mind, then turning away with the doubt unsatisfied. In Lee's case the scrutiny had been sharper. Each time, by some narrow margin, Roderick had withheld comment on his observation, as if he were struggling mightily to be sure—or fair. Roderick was never pleasant company at such times.

So now Lee took his time, letting his father ride ahead through the stiff sage across the flinty ruts of old erosion marks where hoofs raised scant dust.

After a while Roderick looked around. "Don't ride back there like a squaw. I want to talk to you."

They walked the horses side by side. Lee Vail was four inches shorter than his father, who stood six feet two. The son was heavier in the chest and legs, lacking overall the whip-thong litheness of his father. Lee's face was cast in even planes, while Roderick's features were thrust out in an aggressive, hawkish jut. The son's coloring was dark, his hair dark brown, and in those respects he was like his mother. All he had from his father were blue eyes, but they were two shades deeper than Roderick's.

On the scattered ranches of the Sapinero country, an inland empire to itself, it was said that Lee Vail would never be the man his father was; this Lee knew and was content, for he knew, also, that Roderick had paid a price for everything he was and everything he owned.

"Worthless ground." Roderick looked ahead at the empty land, at the humped ridges pouring down from the Fossil Mountains to the north. And then he looked east, toward Kebler and beyond where lay the home ranches of those who had come too late to settle on the south side of the Sapinero. "And worthless people, too." He gave his son a cutting glance. "Are you still running in the brush with Iris Meeker?"

Lee took anger from the blunt question, and then he let the anger die. A fact was so, and, when it was known, it must be accepted. He was calm when he said—"Yes."—and then he watched the surge of fury in his father's face.

"What kind of marriage would that be?"

"We haven't talked of marriage."

"What else would she have in mind?"

Lee said: "I'm well past twenty-one, so let it be."

Roderick's eyes narrowed, and then, surprisingly, he smiled, but it was a taut grimace that went flat in an instant. "A tumble in the hay now and then . . . that's all right. You'd be a stale, miserable man if you didn't get around some when you have the chance. That isn't what I wanted to talk about, anyway." The sweep of Roderick's hand took in a quarter of the compass east and north. "Worthless land, Lee, and worthless people. It's a combination that threatens a man."

The gesture was too dramatic, Lee thought, the words high-flown, except that Roderick's violent background and his present grim intentness gave a dangerous edge to both the movement and the statement. Lee was uneasy. He always was when caught in the swirl of one of his father's driving moods.

"The people are all right," Lee said. "Just because they didn't get here as early as you did. . . ."

"They're all right . . . if you keep them in their place."

Lee stared at his father. "The Crawfords, the Meekers, Joe

Emmett, the Roods . . . all the rest of them on the north side of the river . . . what's got into you suddenly?"

"It's not sudden. You kill trouble before it gets a good hold." Roderick looked south across the Sapinero, toward his Broken Diamond. Calvin Houghton's Two Teepees was the only ranch on that side of the river. "Cal is figuring on starting something, and then the others will take it up." He was so savage and sure that Lee was startled.

Before he met Lee's mother, Roderick had been a ruthless marshal in a trail town. Bits of that history had seeped from him while Lee was growing up. Ten men killed . . . never give a son-of-a-bitch who's after you an even chance.

Lee swallowed against a pressure welling up in his throat. "Start what?" he asked. "Why would Houghton . . . ?"

"He's started already. In Union Park."

The park was Diamond's stronghold, a great bowl that foamed with aspen thickets. Without apparent depletion of the forage, Roderick ran three thousand cattle there year after year. Yesterday, Sam Harvey, the Diamond foreman, had ridden down for supplies, mentioning that he had seen a few head of Teepee's stuff the week before on Ballou Creek.

"You mean those strays?" Lee asked incredulously. "There's always been a few head of Houghton cows wandering in the park.

"Call them strays," Roderick said. "Let them keep coming year after year and then some of the dry-land loafers on this side will get ideas."

Yesterday, when Harvey had dropped the news casually, Roderick had appeared undisturbed. Now, after a day and a half, he was on the warpath. It did not make sense, for in most things Roderick acted on impulse.

Lee said: "It can't be just those few stray cows. What else . . . ?"

"That's damned good and plenty."

"You could have seen Houghton last night at home." That was the proper way. Houghton was hot-tempered, blunt, but a good neighbor, deserving privacy in this matter.

"He'll be at church today," Roderick said. "Him and most of the two-bit ranchers from this side. We'll make it clear to all of them in one whack."

"That's a poor way to do things."

"It bothers you, does it?"

"Yes."

"Why?"

"It's not a public affair. Your way doesn't make sense."

"Afraid?" Roderick asked.

"That's got nothing to do with it. If you insult Houghton and all the rest, you're deliberately asking for their hatred. Not that they ever loved us anyway, but why invite trouble?"

"They'll do nothing. They're afraid. We'll show them how the boar ate the cabbage, and that'll be the size of it."

"I don't like it," Lee said.

"Ann Houghton, huh?"

"No. It's just that you're making a mountain out of a molehill."

"By God, you always were a bear for arguing!"

Lee met his father's hot look squarely. After a time Roderick looked away, pointing this time across the river to where the Razor Mountain lay misty in the afternoon sun. "There were only a few of us here when they started snipping at me in Union Park. It wasn't much at first, just a steer now and then, but it could have built up to something big. I warned the prospectors and drifters that used to hang out around the park. The stealing went right on, so I got old Cannon Ridgway and his crew. We took care of things. There's never been any trouble in the park since. If a man can't see the lesson in that, he's a fool." Roderick looked at his son with a waiting expression that demanded confirmation of the principle he had drawn.

Lee knew. History was brief in the Sapinero country. Acts of violence were the great rocks that stood high in the meager stream of living, and that was why time was still marked from the day Roderick and Cannon Ridgway, now dead, had taken a crew into Union Park and hanged four men for stealing cattle. Whispers ran yet around the deed: that one of the men had been innocent, that the other three had taken an occasional beef for food only.

"We settled the trouble before it had a chance to be fair started." Roderick still waited for his son to speak. When Lee said nothing, the father turned away with anger thin across his face.

Trouble was a chain that grew its own links, Lee thought. It was not broken by one hard smash. Friends of some of the hanged men had come to the Diamond by night three years later. Lee knew nothing of them until the crash of pistols and the slam of a rifle wakened him.

When he ran into the yard that night, Roderick was standing half dressed near the lantern pole. The pale starlight showed him with a pistol in his hand, stooped, unmoving, and on the ground there laid two figures. One of them was making queer bubbling noises and waving his knees from side to side. From the shadows of the porch Lee's mother cried: "Lee! Get away from there!"

Roderick turned slowly, the pistol still at arm's length against his thigh. With less force than his wife, he said: "Go in the house, Lee. Go back to bed. . . ."

Until he fell asleep much later, Lee heard his parents talking in the living room, and then for the first time in his life, he heard his mother crying. When he rose in the morning, he did not try to make a dream of the night. He walked into the yard and looked at the ground near the lantern pole. Someone had shoveled dirt on the place, but Lee saw the flies scrabbling thickly over something in the dust.

Roderick was gone then. The three Diamond riders had been in the hills for weeks. Alone with his mother, Lee tried to find out what had happened, but all Maureen Vail would tell him was that three men had come to hang his father, and then she drew within herself and did not hear his questions. She would not let him out of the house any more.

Sometime in the morning, Roderick returned with old man Ridgway and another rider. Lee saw them take two tarpaulin-shrouded bundles from the barn, and later he saw them digging a half mile away on the hill. Mrs. Ridgway arrived by herself in a buckboard about that time. She stayed a week at Diamond.

Ridgway and his rider left right after dinner. When they were saddling up, Lee heard his father say: "Do you suppose we ought to go after the third?"

Old man Ridgway laughed shortly. "Two out of three is a fair showing. If you want a perfect score, go ahead."

"I guess not," Roderick said. "Thanks for the help, boys." He walked away almost aimlessly.

Ridgway was mounting when his rider said: "He's hell on wheels, ain't he? How many does this make for him?" His voice was full of admiration that sickened Lee.

Ridgway had settled himself in the saddle, a red-faced man with bitter little eyes. He gave the rider a sour look. "Yeah, he's hell on wheels, all right," he said, and then Ridgway went out of the yard on the run.

For several days Roderick was soft and patient with his wife, doing small things for her that Lee had never seen him do before. Mrs. Vail had become unusually quiet, and there were times when she was oblivious to the talk around her. She stirred restlessly about the house at night, often coming into Lee's room to stand silently beside his bed. He pretended sleep when he knew she was there. She began to ride at night, throwing a saddle on a horse and leaving while Roderick's voice followed her, trying to argue her out of going.

Lee remembered yet the sounds of her horse thudding away as if desperation drove her. He seldom heard her return, for she always came in quietly. And then there was a night when she did not return.

He was thirteen then. His father hauled him out of bed in the chill pre-dawn. It was sunup when they found Maureen Vail lying in the rocks of Stormy Ridge where her horse had been spooked and thrown her. She was conscious. She had no broken bones, but her back was injured. Her face was white. Her black hair gleamed against the nest of jagged rocks. She had looked at Roderick and said: "Leave me alone. Go away. I don't want to go back."

Roderick shot a swift look at his son. High willfulness was in his cold, blue eyes, and anger. "She's out of her head, Lee." He had lifted his wife. She had stared at him as if she hated him. Roderick had carried her down the hill to a meadow they could reach with a wagon.

Her horse was grazing there. It came trotting toward them, whickering, holding its head to the side to keep from stepping on the dragging reins. Even yet, Lee remembered the white blaze on its forehead just touched by the rising sun. It was an ugly little horse, short-barreled and strong. Maureen Vail loved it.

Roderick had shot it between the eyes even as his wife cried out against the act. A fiery look that Lee had not seen in a long time brought color to his mother's face. She had cursed Roderick and tried to sit up, but pain had whipped her across the body and drove her head back on Roderick's coat.

This time it surely was hatred in her eyes, Lee had thought.

"I don't want to go back," she had said.

One hind leg of the horse was raking through the heavy dew on the grass, and then it was quiet. Roderick had put his pistol away. "She's out of her head, Lee." He had looked at the horse. "When something you trust lets you down, there's the answer. Remember it, Lee."

The years had washed across the memory, fading Roderick's part to something that now seemed falsely dramatic, but the coloration of Maureen Vail's part was still strong. Lee never saw her in another outburst against his father, so in time he glossed her action over with: *She's out of her head, Lee.*

About the time Sam Harvey came to the Diamond, there was a change in Mrs. Vail. She emerged from behind her shield and faced the world again, visiting around the country, driving to socials, asking people to call at Diamond. That lasted only a brief time, and then she resumed her quiet life at home, but afterward Lee seemed to sense a fire beyond her outer bearing, a desperation that threatened to break through. Then gradually she withdrew, and the curtain closed before her again.

Harvey had nothing to do with any of it, Lee decided. Harvey's arrival was merely a mark in time. He was the only man who had ever worked more than one year for Roderick.

Riding now toward Kebler with Roderick, Lee was puzzled that he should be remembering old events and trying to link them with the present.

"I said I settled things in the park before they had a chance to get out of hand." Roderick stared at Lee, and his statement was an oblique command for Lee to speak.

Settled trouble? No, started it. A direct line stemmed from the hanging in Union Park. It was clear enough to Lee; he thought it should be plain, also, to Roderick.

"You heard me," Roderick said.

Lee studied his father's face. Except for the lack of mustache it was little changed from the wedding picture of him standing tall and tight-lipped beside Lee's mother. Even then, a pistol showed under his long coat. The reason for today was somewhere deep in Roderick's nature, beyond Lee's understanding. Maybe it was that a pistol man could never rest, that the recoil of his weapon carried deep into him and bruised him into new violence. Whatever the reason, there was a price; the demand in Roderick's manner showed that he was paying some of it now, for a man who knows he is right does not seek affirmation of his actions.

Lee made his comment slowly. "It was different when you came here. Maybe you had to be hard, and quick with a rope or pistol then, but now. . . ."

"People never change. They get manners. They build a church, but they cheat and steal as much as ever. They'll run over you, if they can."

"Nobody's trying to run over you!"

"We're serving notice about the park, Lee. Go home if you don't like it." It was the final statement. Roderick quickened the pace of the tall buckskin.

11

The town lay on a flat above the cañon where Silver Creek plunged into the Sapinero. It was named for big Pete Kebler, who had built the first structure, a saloon and general store. Some people still recalled that Roderick had been enraged because the place had not been named for him.

A working man for all his size, and with unusual ideas, Kebler had plowed two furrows a hundred feet apart and a quarter of a mile long to mark the street. Into these he had laid the slender trunks of budding cottonwoods, so that now the single street was a wide and shady lane so thickly lined with trees that the few buildings at the lower end of the town were almost masked. Completely apart from the ten structures, a white-painted church stood at the upper end of the street, and that had also been built largely because of Kebler's efforts.

As soon as Roderick and Lee came off the hot mesa and into the street, Lee felt the violation of their presence strongly. It was Sunday and the one day of the month when the circuit preacher came across the Fossils to hold services: a sermon in the morning and more preaching in the evening. Between times, those who had ridden into town to attend the services gathered to visit and eat lunches in the cool grove behind the church.

Roderick went down the middle of the street. His high cheek bones and narrowed eyes made him look like an arrogant Indian chief on his way to council. There was something obscene, Lee thought, in his desire to knife his will into the quiet afternoon. The door of Kebler's store was open, but no one was in sight. The saloon would be locked since it was Sunday.

Lee said: "I can go up to the grove and tell Houghton you want to see him."

Roderick reined in quickly. "What are you afraid of?" The studying expression was in his eyes. He drew his pistol and checked it. "Look at your gun."

"What for?"

"Check it, damn you!"

"No."

"I've spent time and money teaching you how to handle a pistol. You mean you wouldn't back me up?"

"It's not going to come to that. Nobody wears a gun to town, but if they did, they're in Pete's place now." Lee saw the anger pulse high in his father's face. "I can go tell Houghton to come here."

"Sometimes I wonder if. . . ." Roderick's fury almost exploded into words. He studied the even set of his son's face, and then he rode on.

They passed Mell Crawford's harness store. From there to the head of the street there was nothing but the trees and ditches spilling in and out of water boxes set for houses that had never been built. Soon the murmur of voices came from the grove behind the church.

Lee saw Iris Meeker first. She was sitting on a log bench with Tony Alarid, beyond the long plank tables where the married women chatted. She was a strong woman, wide-hipped, full in the bosom. Even in the shade her hair made a bright, golden shine. She gave Lee a slow smile, and then she looked at Alarid, who was watching Roderick without expression.

The men were scattered around the grove. Gramps Rood was sleeping on a blanket under a tree, his hands folded on his chest, his mouth a round hole in his bushy gray beard. The largest group of men stood or squatted in a circle where Joe Emmett was drawing on the ground with a stick and talking about an easy trail across the Fossils.

George Cantonwine came forward as Roderick and Lee dismounted. He was a tall man whose skin fitted like loose clothes. He misquoted the Bible freely in his sermons, but he spoke with such fervor of hellfire and damnation that his listeners forgot the defect. Even in normal conversations, his voice was a promise of punishment. There was no meekness in Preacher Cantonwine, who rode back and forth across the mountains monthly on a powerful stallion with a misshapen jaw. He fixed Roderick and Lee with a deep-set look, noting their pistols. The slashes in his loose cheeks pinched in as he said: "Welcome to the gathering, brothers. Where's Missus Vail?"

Maureen Vail had not left the Diamond in years, and Cantonwine was aware of that. Roderick said curtly: "She's not feeling well." He looked around the grove. Cal Houghton was not in sight. His wife was sitting at one of the tables.

"On the Lord's day, it would seem that Missus Vail might . . . ," Cantonwine began.

"She doesn't feel a damned bit better then." Roderick did not look at the preacher.

Lee watched the tightening, the exchanged glances, the protective bunching around the rupture he and Roderick had made in the peaceful scene. Joe Emmett tossed his stick away and straightened up. Tony Alarid sat where he was stretching his legs. He hooked his thumbs into his belt and cocked his head, watching the Vails with a half smile on his dark, sharp features.

He was Cal Houghton's foreman. He had hated Roderick Vail since the day he rode into the country and asked for a job at Diamond. Roderick had looked at his rig, listened to his drawl, and then told him bluntly that no Texan would ever work at Diamond. Before he caught on with Houghton, Alarid had worked for Landon Crawford. He fancied himself around Iris Meeker, taking her to dances and socials and church, until the day he came upon her and Lee, high on Gothic Creek. Alarid made his own guess, which happened to be right, and then there were two Vails he hated. As tangible as weight, his attitude carried across the space to Lee.

Lee watched Roderick and saw a moment's hesitation, a tiny balancing that a man who is afraid or careful makes before a critical move. It seemed that way, but neither fear nor carefulness was a quality of Roderick Vail.

Cantonwine said: "Your weapons, my friends, they do not fit the day, and since you seldom see fit to come. . . ."

"Be quiet, Cantonwine," Roderick said.

Anger spouted from the preacher's eyes, a rage fit to call upon the heavens for destruction, but it curdled off and shaded into temporal fear. Lee looked away from Cantonwine, ashamed by the man's breaking. The biting order had raised resentment in everyone. Only Tony Alarid seemed detached from the general feeling. His faint smile was as much contempt for the silence of the men as it was hatred of the Vails.

"Where's Houghton?" Roderick demanded.

Mrs. Houghton rose from a table, a stocky woman, gray-haired and brusque. "What do you mean, coming here and asking for Cal, or any other man, in that tone? That weapon on your hip gives you no right to be here at all." She glanced at Lee and lumped him into the challenge.

"I seek no trouble, Nettie," Roderick said.

Shamed by a woman, Cantonwine tried to regain position. "Your weapon, Vail. I demand. . . ."

Roderick knocked Cantonwine aside with his arm. "Where's Houghton?"

"At the creek," Mrs. Houghton said. "You. . . ."

Roderick said: "Bring him here, Lee."

Alarid's lazy voice was an insult. "Go on, Lee, do your errand." Iris Meeker jogged Alarid with her elbow. He raised one brow and smiled.

Cantonwine's face was a mask of hell, barely contained. He was pale, and his lips were jerking.

"Get Houghton," Roderick said to his son, who had not moved.

The problem solved itself. Houghton and Pete Kebler came from the trees, laughing, talking. Houghton was carrying one of his grandsons on his shoulders. Kebler was a huge, smooth-faced man with shrewd horse-trading sense written all over his features. He caught the full force of the scene before Houghton did. He hoisted the boy clear of the other man's shoulders and the movements of the child's legs raised Houghton's thin, red hair in untidy wisps.

"Been waiting for you, Cal," Roderick said.

Houghton's small eyes gleamed with a sharp intelligence as he walked forward swiftly. He was a round sort of man who rolled in the saddle when he rode. His nose was a small fixture set tightly to his facial bones, his mouth small, thin-lipped. He glanced at Lee briefly as he passed, and then walked up close to Roderick. "What's sticking in *your* craw, Vail?"

Although Houghton was unarmed, Lee recognized a forthright power in the man that would be unaffected whether he wore a pistol or not. Again Roderick hesitated, and Lee hoped he was realizing how foolish he was. Then Roderick said: "There's too many of your cows in Union Park, Houghton."

For an instant, Houghton's face was blank. He looked like a man who set himself for a heavy blow and then been lashed by a string. His eyes bunched at the corners and he said, puzzled: "What's got into you?"

"I said too much of your stuff is wandering into Union Park."

Houghton was no longer off balance. His temper flickered all over his face. "I'm glad you call it wandering, Vail."

"Let it go at that," Roderick said. He swept his gaze on all the men. "I'll take it unfriendly if I see any brand but Diamond even close to the park from now on."

Tony Alarid shook his head gently.

Bliss Rood said: "You're taking it unfriendly now, Vail. Since I been in this country, I never knew of anything from this side to stray a mile on your side of the river." Rood was a squat man, dark-browed. His neck rose from his body in a brief, powerful run. His ears were small and flat, his arms so short they appeared to be held away from his body as if he had stones under his armpits. "You're inviting unfriendliness," he said.

He looked to no one for support. Little Ben Meeker was standing next to him. Ben stared at the ground quickly, as if the act somehow would remove him from Rood.

Roderick looked hard at Bliss until Houghton said: "How many of my head up there?"

"Too many," Roderick answered. "Let Alarid count them when Harvey shoves them out on Cannibal Mesa, three days from now!"

The sides of Houghton's neck were pulsing. "I've got no use for a man who makes a show of everything he does. By Christ. . . ."

Cantonwine cleared his throat. "If you have no other business here, Mister Vail, I suggest. . . ."

"Save your wind," Roderick said. "Come on, Lee."

"Go on, Lee," Alarid mimicked. He rose from the bench. "Trot along at the tail of the old he-lion. Or would you care to take off the pistol and stay a while?"

The challenge was a welcome lift to resentful men. They raised their heads and studied Lee. Cantonwine wanted to speak, but a moist cruelty showed in his eyes, and he was silent.

Pete Kebler said: "That won't help anything, Alarid."

Almost together, two men said: "Shut up, Pete."

Alarid brushed past the big storekeeper and came toward Lee. "Take off the pistol. Stick around. Maybe we can have a special service for you, Lee."

Someone hurrying forward to get a better look stepped on Gramps Rood's leg. The old man woke up and yelled: "What the God damn' hell here!" He sat up and caught the drift of affairs, still cursing. If Preacher Cantonwine heard, he did not bother to rebuke.

A stubbornness he did not try to reason with held Lee where he was. This was the shape of things that came from seeking trouble. Lee resented the fact more bitterly than he did the personal challenge. He glanced at Roderick. The fierce expression on the high-boned face shouted: *Fight him!*

Iris Meeker shoved in beside her father. Her eyes were bright, darting from Lee to Alarid. She ran her tongue along her lips and watched with happy anticipation, her attitude adding weight to the disgust Lee felt about the situation.

"Well?" Alarid said loudly, smiling.

Lee shook his head.

"Hell!" Cal Houghton said. "I never thought it, but I guess it's so." He looked deliberately past Lee to someone standing behind him. Lee followed the glance. Ann Houghton, Cal's daughter, was there, a tall woman with hair like dark copper. She watched Lee so steadily he could not tell what was in her mind. He had thought he knew her, that someday he might marry her, but now she was like the others here who stood apart and set themselves against the Vails.

Suddenly she mattered more than all the rest. Lee wanted her to give some sign to tell him that she knew why he did not want to plunge into a senseless fight. Ann Houghton kept looking at him quietly, and then she walked around the semi-circle of men behind Alarid.

Joe Emmett said: "You're wasting time, Alarid."

"Give him what he asked for, Lee," Roderick said.

The forces twisting Lee were not of his own making. He heard and saw, but nothing in him stampeded away from logical thought. His father's voice still lay on him with brutal authority. The faces behind Alarid taunted him. He caught glimpses of Ann, walking swiftly toward the tables where the women still sat. For just an instant, he felt savage enough to step into Alarid without trying to reason out the motive, but he turned suddenly and went to his horse. Gramps Rood cursed in disappointment. The stinging slap of laughter followed Lee. Cantonwine regained his voice and boomed: "Let us sing 'Shall We Gather at the River'!"

Moments later the singing of the women came thinly, mingled with the heavy tones of man talk and laughter.

Roderick's buckskin came up beside Lee with a surge. "You ruined everything! They're laughing."

"You made the quarrel with Alarid, not me."

Roderick's fury was strained like a tight wire. "You backed out of a fight. You shamed me!"

Roderick had never backed down from a man. Lee recalled clearly how his father had probed at the courage of every man who ever worked at Diamond, testing, picking at them even when he knew they were afraid of him.

Lee said: "You made an enemy of Houghton and every other man there. I don't know your reason, but I had no cause to roll in the dirt with Tony Alarid."

"You made a fool of me!"

That was so. Lee knew his act had turned the edge of the whole affair against them, after Roderick had held the dominant rôle. They rode another hundred feet before Roderick spoke again. Suddenly he threw the buckskin against Lee's horse and crowded the bay around. "Go back there and fight him!"

For a second time that day the time gap between Roderick's thinking and decision troubled Lee. "No," he said. "That would only make it worse."

Roderick's face was blotched red and white. "You're afraid of him."

"No."

"You're gutless, damn you! I've wondered about it, and now I know."

So that was what had been in Roderick's mind during the moments of moody appraisal. Lee said: "I won't go back just to please you."

Roderick's long arm flashed across the space between the horses and the flat of his hand rocked Lee's head sidewise. "I've raised a coward. So help me, Christ. I've spawned a miserable coward!"

The affair in the grove had poured its poison into Lee, the turning away when he knew what it would cost him, but he knew what it had also cost his father, and so he strove to make a balance.

His father struck him again, and all Lee's logic splintered. He leaned out in the saddle and smashed his fist into his father's face. The blow reached only at the end of its power, but it snapped Roderick's head back. The bay jostled nervously when Lee tried to strike again. His father caught his wrist. The two men tugged awkwardly across the space until Lee's horse sidled off and dragged him from the saddle.

Lee clung to his father, trying to pull him down. The buckskin braced itself against the unbalanced weight, standing like a rock. His face contorted savagely, Roderick kicked out of the stirrups and let his weight come down on Lee. They crashed to the ground, Roderick on top.

Still the buckskin held, its eyes rolling, its hindquarters trembling when the struggling men threshed against its legs.

In rough and tumble, Lee's strength was greater than his father's. He hammered Roderick's face with the sides of his fists. He jolted him with the heel of his hand and jarred him loose and tried to get on top of him. Roderick rolled away and leaped up.

There was dust on Roderick's face, a streak of blood at the corner of his mouth. His hat was gone and his tawny hair hung wildly. "Come on," he said. For the first time in his life, Lee saw the full hellfire of a pistol fighter's eyes, a joyous, deep, and evil expression.

He went in at Roderick, swinging heavily. The powerful blows found nothing. Roderick's fists came straight, cracking into his son's mouth, against his cheek bones. Lee's left eye went blind with water. He tried to beat his father's long arms aside and walked straight ahead, into a spearing blow that made his knees hinge. Weaving on his feet, Lee still held stubbornly to getting in close.

With his one good eye centered on Roderick's belt buckle, he rushed. Roderick side-stepped, jamming the heel of his hand against Lee's shoulder. Lee staggered and plowed into the dust on hands and knees. He scrabbled around to face his father, rising to rush in once more. Roderick knocked him flat with one clean blow.

There was nothing but a tall blur before Lee when he got up. He lunged uncertainly toward it. His father drove him back and back with crackling blows until the last one dumped Lee on his backside in the ditch, with one hand resting limply on a water box.

Lee heard his father breathing gustily. He could see him only vaguely, but there was a necessity to rise and go at him some more. Lee tried and could not make it. The blocked water of the ditch rose across his thighs. His arms burned with fatigue and almost did not obey him when he scooped water from his lap and threw it against his face.

Roderick walked away. He smoothed his long hair back with his hands, picked up his hat, and put it on. He found his pistol and spent a few moments blowing dust from it. For a short time he stood by the buckskin, looking at his son. Then Roderick Vail swung up easily and rode out of town.

The singing in the grove was just ending when Lee crawled from the ditch. He saw his horse standing in the shade on the other side of the street and started the long, uncertain trip toward it. He scuffed over his hat and nearly fell when he bent to pick it up. When he reached the bay, he leaned against it, wondering if he could mount.

It was then he saw Alarid and Iris Meeker standing near the church, watching him. Lee picked up the reins and walked, slowly but straight, out of town.

111

After the evening preaching, the women went home in spring wagons, with most of the men riding behind in a loose group. Preacher Cantonwine was beside the Crawfords' wagon. He would spend the night with them and go back across the mountains in the morning. He rode bowed forward slightly, like a man contemplating the evils of the world and how to combat them. Pale moonlight made deep troughs of the furrows in his cheeks. There was a hot rage in him yet, for he was not a forgiving man and this afternoon he had been sorely affronted.

Roderick Vail was a killer, a man with a long record of violence. His wife was high and mighty and would not come to church. She had an Irish name. Cantonwine had never seen her, but now he wondered darkly if there was an altar with heathen images in her home. In time the Lord might punish both her and Roderick, but there was meager satisfaction in the thought. Preacher Cantonwine preferred punishment to be swift and visible and under his control.

Other men would call it revenge for an insult, but Cantonwine considered himself an instrument of the Almighty. One flaw kept fracturing his cankerous thoughts: he was mortally afraid of Roderick Vail.

He rode bent forward in thought, but still he was sensitive to every action of the dangerous horse under him.

"The sermons were wonderful, Reverend Cantonwine," Mrs. Landon Crawford said for the third time.

"The Lord directed my tongue." Cantonwine balanced a line of action against his fear of Roderick Vail. The son was craven; perhaps it would be better to deal with him. It might be possible. But there was still the fear. . . .

Moonlight touched bits of metal among the riders behind the wagons. Their conversation came unevenly. When the wagons were not grinding over rocks, Cantonwine could hear just what was said back there. It was Ben Meeker who was talking now.

"Some big fellow always pushing a man around. It's the same wherever you go. I've made four starts, and it was the same every time. Once in the panhandle. . . ."

Joe Emmett listened to Meeker's whine with pure disgust. Old Ben had been here early enough to take up the best land north of the Sapinero, and with normal effort he could have held the best range, but he had let things drift away from him. Right now, the damned old fool ought to be worrying about his youngest daughter riding home with Tony Alarid. Emmett was worrying about it plenty, but it was not his place to do anything.

"Then I went on out to Kansas . . . ," Ben Meeker continued.

The wagons crossed McGraw Wash, and Ben Meeker reached his fourth start on the Sapinero. The others heard the sound he made and that was all.

Bliss Rood interrupted suddenly without offending Ben or anyone else: "Vail had no call to do that."

"Vail's like that," Chauncey Meeker said. "He was aiming at Houghton, but he had to make a holy show of it." The dim light fell on Chauncey's square jaw and the big white teeth as he spoke. He was Ben's oldest son, a hard-working man who had pulled away from the family after their arrival in the Sapinero country. His ranch was small and his range uncertain, but everything he did was planned with an eye to the future.

"He aimed at all of us," Rood said. He spoke with stubborn anger. "Just for the hell of it, I'd like to dump about three hundred head into Union Park to see how tough he really is. I never heard anything about Roderick Vail until I came here. I like to judge a man first-hand, not from what I hear about him. I'd just like to see what he'd do if someone dropped a few hundred head into that paradise he thinks he owns."

They dipped into the wash and the hoofs of their mounts clopped softly for a time.

Landon Crawford said: "You'll think about that dumping business twice, won't you, Bliss?"

There was a short laugh.

"He brought the idea up," Bliss said. "Nobody has ever bothered him over there. He must be afraid more than he ought to be, to bust out with a warning for no reason. Just what would he do if some of us pushed cows into Union Park? He don't own one foot of that ground."

175

"He might do plenty," Chauncey said. "Him and Sam Harvey. I'd as lief take a chance on Vail as I would Harvey."

"All right, they're both tough." Rood's slow, stubborn speech was like that of a man musing aloud. "We know that. I saw Vail today and I ain't saying I'd care to tackle him in a pistol scrap, and I ain't even sure Lee was afraid of Alarid, like most of you seem to think. But I still ain't sure of just what he could do if a bunch of us started to run cattle in Union Park."

"You started it yourself," Chauncey said dryly, "and now you've got all of us in Vail's pasture."

Once more there was a quick laugh.

"I didn't say I figured to be the first, or even at all." Rood's even tone was unchanged. "But when a man, any man, come dusting in at me with his hair on end and slaps me across the chops for nothing, then, by God, I get to wondering what I can do to pay him back. Nobody's ever bothered Vail, not since I been here. Why should we take anything off him?"

It was almost tangible in the night, the silent agreement with the principle Rood had stated, but the silence also said that no man cared to take it further. Joe Emmett, for one, found logic in the words, but he was not greatly interested. He ran a few cattle, but his main concern was his sawmill on Gothic Creek, and at the moment a greater concern was what Iris and Tony Alarid were doing back there in the night. He looked over his shoulder. When he turned, he sensed that Chauncey Meeker was watching him.

"I don't care about being insulted," Rood said. "I'll figure out something."

"You had your chance," Landon Crawford said. "Alarid. . . ."

"Alarid!" Rood spat the word. "He's a bigger show-off than Roderick Vail. The main question was about Union

Park, and not who's the best man at knocking out some-body's teeth before the ladies."

There was in that an economy of thought, direct, brutal, and disturbing. It put a thinking silence on everyone but Ben Meeker.

"Always pushing a man around," he muttered. "Every time I start, someone like Vail is around to ruin things. I guess he wants everything over here, too." He cleared his throat and even that sound was a whine. "That's the size of it, boys. He wants everything."

They examined that thought and found little substance in it. The wagons bumped on through the sage, sending back a dust odor as bitter as smoke. Cantonwine's stallion spooked and went back jumping through the moonlight until Cantonwine sawed him around and brought him under control.

Crawford said: "Handles that big brute easy-like, don't he?"

Chauncey Meeker had a second side glance at Emmett turning to peer behind.

After another hundred yards, still on the primary subject, Rood asked: "You haven't said a word, Emmett. What do you think?"

"I'm hard to insult," Emmett said. "That seems to be the big bone you're growling over. I ain't much interested in Union Park myself, but if I was, I'd do something about it without a pile of talk."

Rood turned his blunt head and stared a long time through the shifting layers of moonlight at Emmett.

When they came to Gothic Creek, Emmett said good night curtly and rode toward his sawmill. Soon afterward the Crawfords turned toward the river. Cantonwine answered someone's question when the wagon was fifty yards away.

"Yes, sister, he was bold and prideful with his weapon on him, but we must find forgiveness for Roderick Vail and all his kind. Of course, pride goeth before a fall."

When Chauncey Meeker came to his road, he went to the wagon where his mother was and said something. Then he rode down the back trail at a trot, and everyone knew he was going back to check on his sister.

Lee Vail was almost to the river before he noticed that his pistol was gone. It was probably lying in the street in Kebler. He crossed the Sapinero at Island Ford where the water was scarcely knee-deep on the bay. On the far side he undressed and bathed in the icy current. It was mainly his face. His lips were cut and swelling, one eye was closed, and his lower jaw moved on its hinges painfully.

He had no pity for himself; he merely wondered how he had lived so long without knowing certain things about his father. He shook the dust from his clothes and dressed. Then he sat beside the riffle, flipping pebbles idly, while a corner of his mind resisted the idea of going home. At last he got the bay from the willows.

The hills broke down to flatness beside the river where Diamond lay. For a mile the Sapinero ran slowly beside meadows that were sub-irrigated by warm springs that made a great white fog in winter. The ranch buildings were not large or many, for Roderick employed only three riders in summer and but one in winter.

All around the house were white-sand walks and planter walls of hard, red rock; these things Maureen Vail had built with her own hands since her slow recovery from her accident. Lee rode into the yard reluctantly.

His mother and Sam Harvey were sitting on the porch. When Mrs. Vail had a look at Lee's face as he was dismounting, she came toward him quickly, a tall, slender woman with jet-black hair. Her eyes were gray, flaky. For a long time they had looked out on life with a detachment that was more than reserve.

"What happened, Lee?" Mrs. Vail was concerned but not disturbed. She had seen her son with broken legs and arms, once with his scalp laid open for six inches and five of his ribs cracked.

"A fight."

"Who with?"

Then Roderick had not come home yet. "With a man. Where's Roderick?"

"With you, I thought. Come in the house and let me fix up those cuts."

"They'll be all right." Lee paused uncertainly. He had expected her to know about the trouble, and now he did not want to tell her.

"It must have been a tough man, Lee," Mrs. Vail said. "Look at his face, Sam."

"I'm looking." Harvey was still on the porch, standing with one foot on a stone wall. He was a man of medium size. His tight-set, wavy hair had once been red, but now it was grayed to roan. An underlying quietness had compressed upon his face an expression that just missed being blank, but his dark eyes, restless and penetrating, belied the grave composure of his features. Men who met him for the first time often glanced at him and filed him in some standard niche, then looked a second time and were not sure about him.

"Who'd you fight with, Lee?" Mrs. Vail asked. "Joe Emmett?"

Emmet! Then she knew about him and Iris and how Joe Emmett had been left behind. "No," Lee said. "Roderick."

The quick change in his mother amazed him. A boiling violence broke the uncontrolled cast of her face. She glanced at Harvey. "You and Roderick. Why?"

"We disagreed, that's all." Lee tried to find something in Harvey's face. The man looked at him bleakly.

When Lee turned to his mother again, she was walking away. "I'd like some coffee," he said.

She nodded.

Lee led his horse toward the corral. Glancing across his shoulder then, he saw his mother almost running toward the house. Ever since her accident she had not been well, or at least the thought had come to be accepted around the Diamond, and elsewhere, too, because she seldom left the ranch. Yet when Roderick and Lee were in the hills, she had built stone walls and wheeled dirt like a man, and afterward answered Roderick's outraged complaints by saying that she had done it all a little at a time. Frequently she knocked her plaster walls apart and changed the design or moved them. Now Lee remembered that he had seen stones broken as if his mother had gone at her work with some fury driving her.

The knowledge smashed into Lee that there was nothing physically wrong with Maureen Vail and probably had not been for several years, but since that morning he and Roderick had brought her back from Stony Ridge, she had stepped behind the barrier of fragility, seeking protection from something that Lee did not understand. He could not remember that she had promoted the idea in any way, by complaint or by pretense. She had merely allowed what appeared to be a reasonable premise to grow into an accepted fact.

Lee watched her take the porch steps in one stride. Sam Harvey said something to her. She shook her head. The two of them stared at each other for a moment, and then Mrs. Vail went into the house.

Unformed thoughts lay uneasily on Lee's mind as he took care of his horse. Harvey ducked between the corral poles and watched Lee for a while before he spoke.

"He went over to Kebler and called Houghton about the strays in the park?"

Lee glanced sharply at Harvey's impassive face. "How'd you guess that?"

"Saw it coming."

"You know Roderick better than I do."

"I guess." There was meaning all around the edges of the simple statement, like a flickering light that defied identification.

It struck Lee that he did not know the depths of Harvey, either. For six years, the man had been at Diamond, from spring roundup to late fall, spending most of that time in Union Park. He was an old friend of Roderick's, from somewhere. Although Lee had never heard his father and Harvey talk openly and fully of their past, he had heard names and places come together in their talk to prove that they had known each other well before Lee was born.

"He spoke his piece before everyone at the church?" Harvey asked. Faintly, in his choice of words rather than the tone, ran condemnation that raised at once a stiffness in Lee.

"Yes," Lee said. No matter what he thought and Harvey thought, Roderick was not a matter for them to maul over in criticism. "Who told you?"

"No one." Harvey studied Lee quietly. "In case you feel you didn't do very well, I'll say that only one man I ever knew even came close to licking your father in a stand-up fight."

"That part doesn't bother me one bit."

"I know."

Lee slapped his horse away. "You know what?"

"That a licking doesn't bother you."

"I can't say that I care for one."

Harvey nodded. His eyes lighted almost to a smile, but they grew dark in an instant, and he said carefully: "No man cares for a beating, Lee. But it happens to all of us." He seemed to be arranging thoughts, trying to estimate their impact in advance, but whatever it was that he might have added did not come.

"What brought you down today?" Lee asked. It was a casual question, but as it hung unanswered, with Harvey studying him, implications grew and colored the memory of the words.

"I came to get orders to move Houghton's stuff out of the park," Harvey said evenly.

"You knew there would be such orders?"

Harvey nodded. His assurance irritated Lee because it was based on an understanding of Roderick's character that Lee did not have.

Harvey said: "You told Roderick he was making a big mistake?"

"Yes."

"Was the fight before or after he talked to Houghton?"

"After."

"Then there's another reason, too, which is none of my business."

"That means you're curious. All right. I refused a fight with Tony Alarid."

"Alarid? He offered a pistol fight?"

"He wasn't armed."

Harvey glanced at Lee's empty holster. His reaction died away behind some withheld thought. "I'll go back to the park."

"Roderick must have gone straight there from town to tell you to move Houghton's strays."

"Partly that," Harvey said. He did not turn away soon enough to conceal the savage glitter that ran across his dark eyes. "The rest was because he wouldn't have to come home and tell about the fight."

Lee watched him ride across the yard. Maureen Vail came out on the porch. As Harvey passed her, he raised one hand slowly and let it fall, and the gesture was a gentle salute carrying a full measure of communication. Mrs. Vail was motionless, but her eyes followed Harvey's going until he put his long-legged claybank into a trot. It all passed in seconds. A treacherous, disturbing thought ripped through Lee, and he wondered how many times he must have seen a small, sharp moment like this one, without observing anything.

Mrs. Vail said quietly: "The coffee is ready." She said it again before the words struck through to Lee.

Lying sleepless in the middle of the night, Lee heard his father, sliding poles at the corral, later, the long strides in the yard. Lee knew his mother was sitting in the living room. He heard Roderick trying to cross the porch softly. The door opened and closed, and then Roderick said: "Maureen! What are you doing up at this hour?" His voice was heavy with concern. "Good Lord, woman, you're not going to start that all over again, are you?"

"What are you starting, Roderick?"

"Nothing, nothing! There won't be any trouble. Houghton will growl and grunt and that will be the size of it."

"When you and Cannon Ridgway started for Union Park years ago, over something no worse. . . ."

"That was different," Roderick said. "Completely different." His voice was reasonable, persuasive. "Believe me, there won't be any trouble this time. The old days are gone."

"Are they?"

Lee thought of that night long ago when gunfire in the yard had blasted him from sleep. He could picture the doubt and tension on his mother's face. Quietly he rose and slipped into his pants.

Roderick did not answer his wife's question. "Lee here?" he asked.

"He's here."

"Did he tell you about . . . ?"

"That you two fought? Yes."

"I called him a coward. Maureen, I was wrong, but my temper was up, and I couldn't help myself."

There was a long silence. Lee walked into the living room. His mother looked very small and quiet, sitting in a deep chair beside a lamp that was turned low. In spite of the dim light, Roderick made a striking figure, tall and aggressive. Shadows took the harshness from his bony face, but his explosive, driving vitality was still evident in the way he stood, in the way he turned to look at Lee. He said: "You sulking?"

Lee shook his head.

Roderick grinned. He held up his left arm. "You hit me so hard on that arm a time or two, that I could scarcely use it the rest of the day. There was only one thing, Lee . . . you were so mad you were swinging wild." He crossed the room and clasped Lee by the shoulder. "It's not going to happen between us again." He turned to his wife. "Anything around this dump for two fighting men to eat?"

"I can fix something." Mrs. Vail's face lay in the shadows beyond the lamp. Her voice was inexpressive.

"Never mind," Roderick said. "We'll rustle up something. Come on, Lee."

They crossed the room together, Lee's doubts and worries weakening under his father's booming energy and friendliness.

Mrs. Vail said: "There's roast beef in the springhouse. Be sure to wrap the cloth around it good before you put it back."

While Roderick rummaged in the summer kitchen for bread and onions, Lee went through the soft night to the springhouse. He found the roast, and butter, and four bottles of beer in the well where the water ran ice-cold.

On his way back to the house he glanced just once toward the Razors and the mighty pool of blackness that was Union Park. When he walked into the light, he saw that Roderick had taken off his pistol belt. He was slicing onions with a heavy knife.

"Women worry," Roderick said. "That first deal in the park gave her hell afterward, when the three men came here to get me." He stared at the table a moment. "We've got to keep from worrying her, Lee. She's never been well since she took that fall." He flipped the onion slices on a saucer, using the knife like a spatula. "The reason I didn't come straight home from Kebler today was because I was ashamed to face her."

This frank admission of a fact already stated by Sam Harvey helped to still further the lingering unease in Lee.

They ate their food and drank beer, sitting across from each other under the lamp where moths made fluttering runs. Lee felt the last of the troubling uncertainty draining away. This was home, security. He could now remember other times with his father when their relationship had been based on small things as strong and binding as this moment. The remembrance was a tightly woven effect without detail, a force that bound him powerfully to his father.

"Where'd you know Harvey?" Lee asked.

"We were lawmen together in Granada." Something

pricked at Roderick's contented mood, but he pushed the annoyance aside. "You could have stomped Alarid into the ground, Lee. How come you didn't?"

"I was sore at you for busting up the meeting."

"I sure did." Roderick said absently. "They didn't scare one bit, those three." He was darkly thoughtful, chewing his food slowly. "Did you see old Cantonwine's face? I thought he was going to swallow his teeth."

They finished their food and the beer. Since neither of them smoked, they sat only a few moments longer before starting to clean up the mess they had made.

"Harvey is going to run the Teepee's stuff out?" Lee asked.

Roderick nodded. "Won't amount to anything, but it was time to read the law about the park. Every so often, Lee, when they think you are getting soft . . . you'll find out when I'm gone and you're running Diamond."

The thought of his father ever being gone kicked coldly inside Lee.

"Make your peace with Ann," Roderick said. "Better do it in the morning. She'll listen." He was quite sure. "Another thing, you'd best quit sky-shooting around on the north side with Iris and get good and serious over here."

"At least good," Lee said. They grinned at each other, and it was like an arm handshake after much bitterness.

Roderick wrapped up the roast and took the butter. He went out, swearing mildly when he stumbled over some loose stones his wife had gathered for a planter.

Lee went toward his bed. His mother was still sitting in the living room. "You feel all right?" he asked.

"Of course."

"You're just sitting there."

"I'm thinking. I often do."

"Don't worry about the park. Nothing will come of it today."

"I have your father's word for that, also." A bitterness, sensed rather than apparent in Mrs. Vail's voice, made Lee eye her sharply, but he saw nothing, and he guessed that Roderick was right. Women were worriers.

"Good night, Lee."

Lee fell asleep at once, but he woke up some time later when he heard Roderick, almost querulous in his effort to be gentle, telling Mrs. Vail that she ought to go to bed. Once more the currents of things not understood washed coldly against Lee, and he could not recapture the relaxed feeling of a short time before.

He kept seeing his father's contorted face during the fight, and he kept remembering Harvey's almost negligible gesture to Mrs. Vail when the man was riding away that afternoon.

IV

On his way to Two Teepees to see Ann Houghton, Lee met big Pete Kebler riding his thirteen-hundred-pound gray. Kebler's saddlebags were bulging. He was not a man content to let new merchandise sit on his shelves until someone came in to see it; instead, he spent much time riding about the country with samples, and in the process he did favors for everyone. There was nothing servile in Kebler. He liked people.

His shrewd eyes brushed over the marks on Lee's face. "Just headed for your place, Lee. Got some stuff here I think your mother will like."

Lee nodded. Mrs. Vail was always glad to see Kebler. Before his smooth expansiveness she loosened up a little, and sometimes even laughed. An old thought with no clear foundation chased after the first one—Mrs. Vail was always easy and natural in the presence of any man, except Roderick.

"You just come from Houghton's?" Lee asked.

"Yep! I was there for a couple of hours."

"You're an early riser, Pete."

"You know how it is."

Lee grinned wryly. "How's it look for me?"

Kebler shrugged. "She's got a lot of common sense, Ann has." He unbuckled a saddlebag and hauled out a pistol. "Happened to see it in the ditch."

As Lee thrust the weapon under his belt, he observed that it had been cleaned and oiled. "Thanks."

Kebler waved carelessly and rode away.

There were more buildings at Two Teepees than at Diamond, for Houghton, whose range was not largely in one place, needed twice the crew that Roderick Vail needed. Ten years ago, Cannon Ridgway had started to expand Two Teepees, but both he and his wife had died soon afterward. Houghton, a nephew of old Ridgway's, had inherited the place.

Lee rode into the yard and did not dismount.

Houghton came from the house with his rolling, choppy walk. His thin, red hair glinted in the sun. His face was sour, but he was neither bitterly hostile nor friendly when he said: "Well, since you're here, you may as well get down." And then he saw the pistol under Lee's belt. "By God, no! Stay right where you are, Vail. What do you want?"

"I came to see Ann."

Houghton might not have heard. "Tell your father I won't have a crew on Cannibal Mesa to pick up my cattle. They can drift where they damn' well please until I have time to pick them up next fall."

"All right."

Houghton examined the mild answer with suspicion, anxious to quarrel. Before he could get it started, his daughter came out. Ann Houghton's green eyes held lurking fire as she looked at Lee. She, too, was ready for a fight as she came without hurry across the yard, watching Lee's face all the way. The sun brought out the blue squares in the pattern of her gingham dress.

She said without welcome: "Get down, Lee, if you wish."

Houghton growled something and rolled his shoulders irritably. He went with a chopping walk back into the house. Lee walked with Ann to the corner of a log blacksmith's shop out of earshot of the main building. "Roderick might have been over-hasty yesterday, Ann."

Ann glanced at Lee's pistol.

"All right. I was there, but it was against my wishes."

"Was it?" She gave Lee the sharp point of her expression. "Or do you want to dominate everyone you meet, like your father? I've wondered. You've been close at times to asking me to marry you?"

"Yes."

A doubt that might have been based on hurt touched Ann's expression, but there was no softening. "I wouldn't care for a life of building flower beds that I would tear up a week later."

"What do you mean?"

"Just what I said."

Lee grabbed her roughly by the shoulders. "What do you mean?"

Quite close behind Lee, Tony Alarid said: "So you finally found someone you'd fight, huh, Vail?"

As Lee turned, the blow caught him in the corner of the mouth. He raised his arms, and with his hands open he walked at Alarid. Alarid moved back lightly, his smile streaking coldly across his dark face. Lee had learned his lesson about wild rushes; he walked in deliberately. Three or four times Alarid's fists smashed into his battered face.

Then Lee caught the man's wrist and swung around him in a half circle. When Alarid put his furious, wiry strength into a counter tug, Lee let go suddenly. Alarid staggered back. Lee went into him then, crashing his shoulder into the man's chest. They slammed against the corner of the black-smith's shop where the axe-cut log-ends protruded raggedly. A deep, wrenched groan came from Alarid when his spine struck.

Lee hit him once before Alarid slipped sidewise along the building and gained open ground. Alarid showed his hurt. He was white around the mouth, and he carried himself stiffly. But he closed Lee's bad eye with a stabbing blow. He split Lee's swollen lip. He kicked at Lee's groin. The full force of the boot heel crunched against Lee's hips and sent pain wracking through his body.

Limping, Lee closed in until he once more had Alarid by the wrist. With his other hand, he grabbed him above the elbow. Alarid jabbed at his eyes with spread fingers. The nails raked the bridge of Lee's nose and cut to the bone below his left eye. Lee was pivoting then, swinging Alarid. He took the lighter man once around, Alarid's boots scraping at the dirt as he tried to hold his feet. Lee let him go to crash against the shop a second time, so hard that chunks of mud daubing fell from between the logs.

Alarid struck on the point of his shoulder, with his right hand slapping out to break the jolt. Lee was on him then, crowding mercilessly. He sledged Alarid twice in the neck. Alarid's arms came down. His face turned a dirty, olive color. Lee stepped back to get more force into his next blow.

The world turned gray. A shock went down Lee's body,

and his knees almost buckled. He stared numbly at Alarid, wondering how the man had reached him, and then Ann cried: "That's enough!" She was holding a piece of scrap iron in both hands, poised for a second blow. "You don't have to kill him!"

Back to the logs, with his feet dug in hard, Alarid tried to hold up against the sickness in him, but his knees began to weaken. He went down the building in little jerks. He sat on the ground with his knees jackknifed high, staring at Lee.

"Get out of here," Ann said to Lee.

Lee looked another long moment at Alarid. Nothing was settled. They both saw that. Lee turned and limped toward his horse, paying no attention to Cal Houghton, who came running, shouting angrily in a high-pitched voice. Mrs. Houghton, standing in the doorway, watched Lee mount and ride away. Her arms were crossed, her plump brown face stern.

Three miles away, on Vail land, Lee knelt beside a spring to drink. The cold water reflected the picture of a beaten brute, and he kept remembering the disgust that had cut like shattered glass in Ann's voice when she told him to get out.

He rode toward Union Park to find one of his father's camps where there would be no one to talk to. He found nobody at the lower cabin on Steuben Creek, so he stayed there three days and nights, listening to the cool swishing of the wind through the aspens, trying to find solutions to problems that he did not understand.

Long ago he had adopted Roderick's way of going and coming when it suited him, with no thought of explaining to Maureen Vail unless she asked, and now, for the first time in his life, he wondered if she ever worried about his and Roderick's absences.

Pete Kebler found him there near noon of the fourth day.

Kebler's gray was tired, and Pete looked as if he had had enough riding to suit him for a while. "I should have guessed this place first, but I went west to Campton Mesa." There was no shrewdness in the big merchant's face now. He sat for a while as if he did not like the thought of feeling saddle weariness when his feet struck ground. "Your mother sent me," he said, and swung down heavily. "Somebody shot Roderick through the shoulder yesterday at Black Bog." Kebler studied the jolt of his words against Lee.

"Who?"

Kebler shook his head. "He rode in by himself. He fell off his horse in the yard. I showed up about two hours later with some stuff your mother had ordered the other day when I was there." Kebler hesitated. "He'll have a crippled shoulder, Lee."

While Lee was saddling, Kebler waited beside him with the air of a man who has more bad news.

"You'd better rest up here," Lee said. "You've had a hell of a ride."

"Yeah. I'll stay to eat, and then I've got to find Harvey. Somewhere on Ballou Creek, would you say?"

Lee nodded. "My mother asked for him?"

"Yes."

"Say what you're thinking!"

"No need to, Lee. I'll tell you something you don't know. Alarid got into a quarrel with Houghton. Houghton fired him. Alarid went to town. He's spread the word around that he'll wait there for you."

"I won a great victory," Lee said bitterly, "when I hammered that fellow against the blacksmith's shop at Teepees."

"It developed. You couldn't help it." Sympathy that was quickly withdrawn showed on Kebler's smooth face. He walked away to unsaddle his horse.

* * * * *

Roderick was asleep, his face sharp and flushed. Lee stood beside his mother in the bedroom, shocked to see how bony and cruel his father's features looked when the vitality was drained. No emotion, only competence, showed on Mrs. Vail's face. She turned away after a few moments, and Lee followed her into the kitchen. He closed the door.

"Sam will be along as soon as Kebler finds him. Probably by dark," Lee said

Mrs. Vail nodded absently. "I thought he should know."

"How long have you been in love with Sam Harvey?"

With no trace of surprise, Maureen Vail eyed her son steadily. "Since he first came here, for certain, and possibly long ago, before I married Roderick."

"That's a hell of a thing!"

"Don't I know that?" Mrs. Vail gave Lee a flash of temper he had not seen for a long time. "It might have been someone else, anyone who was many things your father is not. Roderick was born to violence. He seeks it. I thank God that you're not like him."

"Maybe I am."

Mrs. Vail shook her head. "He hanged men who should not have been hanged. He slammed his will against those who were afraid of him, and most men were, and that is worse than outright killing. No, Lee, I have not loved Roderick for a very long time, if I ever did."

"You married him."

"I did." Maureen Vail's regret was a simple, powerful force that snapped across Lee's mind and cooled his anger.

"The whole country knows what I didn't guess," he said.

"I suppose. Pete Kebler knows. Missus Houghton does, I'm sure."

"Ann told me she didn't want a life of building flower beds

that she could rip apart over and over."

"Then she knows."

"You never loved Roderick?" Lee asked.

"I thought I did. Roderick never needed me. Making men fear him, killing them if they didn't . . . that served his appetite best. Do you love Iris Meeker, Lee?"

"No. But what's that got to do . . . ?"

"It's the same. I was offered marriage, but the attitude was no different from the way you regard Iris." Mrs. Vail was matter-of-fact, but underneath Lee sensed the throbbing of a woman who had always been furiously alive. She had been stunned by her mistake, but she had never been beaten down, and her spirit would forever lunge and fight against the contract she had made.

Lee said: "Some say you haven't stuck by him properly."

"That's a man's talk. I've killed for Roderick." Mrs. Vail spoke so quietly that her words came out like hammer blows. "The night the three men came here to hang him when you were little . . . I killed one of those men with a rifle from the porch that night."

Lee saw the stark image of thoughts long-hidden behind the gray eyes. His mind leaped back to things he thought he had forgotten, in days when he had, briefly, been closer to his mother than to Roderick, to the memory of her laughter that had died, and now he saw clearly all the changes that had grown in front of him. Something was torn inside him. Part of him was lost to his mother and much of him to Roderick.

"It's no good having Sam around," he said.

"I know that better than you. But last time he was here, I made him promise to leave this week."

"You've thought of running off with him . . . of getting a divorce."

"Of course I have!" A passionate fire blazed in Mrs. Vail's

expression. "But I never will."

In the long silence Roderick's call came to them weakly. "Lee, where are you?"

"He's never called for me, not once." Mrs. Vail gave her son a bleak look.

They went together to where Roderick lay. His eyes burned hotly. He paid no attention to his wife when she offered him a drink of water. "It was Alarid, Lee," Roderick said.

"You saw him?"

"I saw him. I even marked his saddle with a rifle shot when he was clearing out. Go get him, Lee. Make him crawl, then kill him."

Lee nodded. He turned away, glancing at his mother in mute and miserable acknowledgment of her estimate of Roderick. He went outside and stayed there, watching the trail toward the park until Sam Harvey came riding in at dusk.

"How is he, Lee?"

"All right. Why don't you ask about my mother?"

A queer, hard light gathered in Harvey's eyes.

"Clear out, Sam. Day after tomorrow she'll meet you in Buena Vista."

Harvey's intentness was like the stare of a gun muzzle. "She won't go."

"I'll see to it." Lee said it, and then he believed it. "Don't go in the house. Just leave." He waited, and Harvey did not move. "Go on, damn you!"

There was a hard, deep moment while Harvey balanced something in his mind. He got back on his jaded horse and rode away slowly.

Lee looked up toward Union Park. The trouble had not started there; it had begun, instead, the moment Roderick was born. He was a surging, savage man, and he would not change, but he could be checked by someone who was not afraid of him, by someone who loved him. Lee thought it must be his mother's strength that made him steady now. She had used her strength as patience, and failed. He would use his aggressively, hurling the weight of it against Roderick, as ruthlessly as he had crashed Alarid against a wall, whenever Roderick needed curbing.

After dark, Pete Kebler came in on a horse he had borrowed from a Diamond rider on Ballou Creek. Lee was waiting outside for him.

"Pete, I'm going to Two Teepees," Lee told him. "When I come back, will you drive my mother to Buena Vista in the buggy? She won't be coming back."

Kebler was loosening his cinch. All at once he was dead still, a big, dark shadow in the lantern light.

"I should do it myself, I know," Lee said. "But tomorrow I'm going to town to meet Alarid. Think on it first, Pete. Roderick will never be your friend again."

"All right." Roderick had never been any man's friend, Pete thought. There were ways to get along with him, that was all, and there would be ways even after tonight. Pete knew how to manage. He guessed that Lee would do all right, too, for he remembered how Lee had stood, not stubbornly, but strong and sure, against Roderick's order to fight Tony Alarid last Sunday. Kebler had seen then what others might have missed. Even in rage, Roderick had been afraid of his son's solid will. Roderick Vail would never break Lee; in time the son's steadiness would bend him, instead.

A rare man in that he never held any personal reservation in the pleasure he felt when he believed the uncertain struggle was shaping up well for human beings, Pete Kebler said: "All right, Lee. I'll do that."

* * * * *

Mrs. Houghton answered Lee's hail from a bedroom window and then came to the door with a lamp. Her gray hair was disarrayed from sleeping. She wore a bright blue quilted robe. In time of trouble, she was as sturdy as a stone church. She heard only part of Lee's request before she said: "Harness up my mare."

"Now what the hell does he want?" Houghton grumbled as he came rocking from the back of the house.

"Oh, hush, Calvin," Mrs. Houghton said. "His father has been shot." She disappeared with the lamp.

"Too bad!" Houghton clumped to the door, trying to tuck a flannel nightshirt inside his pants.

Ann's voice called out: "Don't quarrel with him now, Dad! Tell him I'll go with him, too."

"Sure!" Houghton cried. "Hell, yes! Let's shut down everything and ride over to Diamond for a picnic." He stepped outside with Lee. "I had to fire Alarid. Damn you, Vail! You prodded him into getting so mean he thought he could open his yap to me and. . . ."

"I prodded him into nothing. Which corral is Missus Houghton's buggy mare in?"

"By God! You make free of the place right after. . . ."

"She asked me to harness the mare. I didn't come here to quarrel with you," Lee said. "I'll tell you now there will be no declarations about Union Park. I'd like you to forget what Roderick and I said."

"Yeah? Who's talking? You or Roderick?"

"I am. It goes for both of us."

Houghton grunted. "That's an interesting change, if you make it stick." His belligerence ran thin. "Let's get the damned buggy."

They took the short way across the whale-backed hills.

Starlight soothed the land. The night was cold. Lee kept glancing at the women in the buggy, and now he was unsure of himself. He had talked to his mother about going away with Harvey and her answer had been no. He thought Ann and Mrs. Houghton would understand, but he could not ask their help, for there was a basic violation of much that all women stood for in the act he thought best for Maureen Vail.

Half accusingly he said: "You two knew all the time that my mother was in love with Sam Harvey."

They did not answer him.

"I want her to go away with him, to get a divorce," Lee said. "She's been unhappy long enough. But she won't go."

A minute or two later he heard someone crying. Ann, he thought at first, and then he realized it was Mrs. Houghton. He was genuinely puzzled. . . .

Once more Lee paced the yard with his mother, using her own arguments, adding his views. The answer was no. It was mechanical, Lee decided, based on a decision made long ago, but he could not change his mother's mind. She went into the house, and he strode to the barn where Pete Kebler was dozing on a bale of hay. Lee began to unharness the horse, and after a moment Kebler roused up and helped him. Neither man spoke.

It was something that a man like Kebler, who had much to lose by becoming involved in a family affair, had been willing to stand with Lee. It was something to remember well, even though the plan had failed. They hung the harness up and put the buggy horse back in its stall. Kebler said: "I think I'll just stretch out in the hay for the night." He lay down, but he did not go to sleep. "Better get some rest, Lee."

"In a minute." Lee sat down on a bale of hay. The minute ran a long time while he stared at nothing.

Someone came down the yard and pushed the barn door open violently. Mrs. Houghton said: "She'll be ready in fifteen minutes. God help me for talking to her about it."

Kebler sprang up from his resting place.

Lee said: "It's the best thing for her."

"The hell it is!" Mrs. Houghton said. "How would a man know? You've been no better to her than Roderick, most of the time, Lee Vail."

She walked out quickly, and both men knew it was best to let her go without thanks, or without saying anything.

Lee was alone when the buggy wheels whispered away into the night. His last look at Maureen Vail's face had told him that she had known this was right. But there was a price for being right, as well as for being wrong, and Lee knew he and his mother would pay it. Yet he was sure that in time the grip of the frozen years would loosen and Maureen Vail would gain her share of happiness. The price that Lee would pay to Roderick would be harsh but fair. Now there was tomorrow, the day that Lee had rejected until other things were settled.

Ann came out and stood beside him.

"He'll never really miss her," Lee said. "He'll think so for a while." Roderick's wounded vanity would be a terrible force and Lee's major test in the new relationship at Diamond. Quite soberly Lee decided that he would win because he had his father's will, but tempered stronger by his mother's spirit. "You don't think I *want* to meet Alarid tomorrow, do you, Ann?"

"I know better now. I know a great deal about you, Lee."

There was a bright, new moment, unclouded by the past or future, living only on their presence in the pale starlight, but Lee's mind slipped inexorably toward tomorrow and he said: "We'll talk later, Ann."

"There must be a later, remember that."

Ann left him then, half running toward the house. . . .

Lee swung around and rode in from the upper end of the
street because he did not want to see a human target between
him and a church. The rail in front of Crawford's harness
store was crowded with horses, and there were more in front
of Kebler's place.

Gramps Rood saw him first. "Here's Vail!" he yelled in a
high voice. In a moment, men were tumbling from the buildings. Kebler's clerk ran into the street. For some reason he
took off his apron, wadded it up, threw it down, and then he
ran back into the store. Bliss Rood was standing near the harness shop, armed, sullen. Joe Emmett was there, bound by
the moment, but still aloof from those he shared it with.

Lee saw Preacher Cantonwine, who should have been far
across the Fossils by now. Grim and foreboding, Cantonwine
looked upon the scene with the air of a bloodless judge. He
would pray afterward, Lee thought; he would pray with
fervor, if he saw Lee dead.

The face of hatred. Lee dismounted. A man angled out from
the cottonwoods on his right. It was Sam Harvey. Lee gave
him a curious look, and all at once a feeling of terrible loneliness was gone. "She started to Buena Vista last night, Sam."

Harvey nodded gravely. Lee saw in his face what he had
seen in Maureen Vail's eyes. The last link of a doubt was
broken.

"I heard the talk when I came through here last night,"
Harvey said. "So I stayed."

"I have to do it, Sam."

"So will he." Harvey paused. "Did Roderick mention a
bullet mark he might have put in a man's saddle?"

Lee nodded.

"There's one on Alarid's saddle. Take your time, Lee. He's in Kebler's. Let him come to you. Then take your time." Harvey led the horse away, and then he walked casually down the street, stopping short of the group where Bliss Rood was.

Alarid came out of the store quickly. He stopped in the street, glancing at the crowd. He had set up this spectacle, and now he must make the most of it. "I bet the drinks you wouldn't be here, Vail. How'd you stir up the guts to come?"

Lee said nothing. The crowd was silent, and so, no matter what sentiment there was against Lee, the fine edge of Alarid's remark broke and gave him his first small loss. He came forward.

"Your old man must have beaten you into coming. Did he?"

Alarid's last two words had lifted with a faint tinge of fear. Lee waited.

"I hate to shoot a scared man." Alarid came on.

Lee was positive then. A man was talking to fill some hollow in himself. He saw Alarid reach for his pistol. The moment compressed to one sharp point, and then it lost all clearness, for then and afterward.

Lee was deliberate. He aimed and fired, clutching the trigger as carefully as if he were shooting at targets with Roderick behind the springhouse. He saw Alarid jerk around a half step, and then the man fell like a cut rope. Powder smoke drifted back to Lee. A sickness went through him in a great, cold wash. He put his pistol away, staring at the ground.

After a time, Sam Harvey was standing in front of him. "He'll live. When he gets well, he'll clear out." Harvey's face was tightly curious. "How many times did he shoot?"

Lee shook his head negatively. He didn't know.

"Twice. I didn't expect you to take that much time."

Harvey raised his hand to touch Lee's shoulder. Something stopped him. He studied Lee for a moment, then he turned and walked away.

They had carried Alarid into the store, and now he was of no great interest to anyone, but men milled where he had fallen. Lee led his horse to them. He spoke directly to Bliss Rood. "Roderick and I made a mistake Sunday." It was enough to say. Let them think it over and do what they would with it.

After a time some of the sullenness left Rood's face. He milled his thoughts over as slowly as he had chewed on anger. The apology had come to him alone, giving him importance, making him the spokesman for the whole north side of the Sapinero. "It's something to hear a man say that, at least." He looked around at the men near him. "It's something, boys." He stared at Lee. "I guess he means it, too."

Cantonwine was in the doorway of the store when Lee rode away. Lee watched him so steadily that the man's gaze dropped. There was nothing anyone could do about men like this, Lee thought.

The farther Lee got from town, the more his mood lifted. When he came up from the river and struck the first unfenced Diamond meadow, bending to a soft wind from the Razors, he saw a tall woman riding toward him like a demon. Her hair was burnished copper in the sun. The moment that lived last night came clean and strong once more. Tomorrow could not harm it.

He put his horse into a gallop.

WILL COOK

UNTIL DAY BREAKS

North Texas, 1870. For three years a delicate peace has existed between the U.S. Army and the Comanche, led by Quanah Parker. The architect of this peace, General Tracy Cameron, has given an impassioned speech in Washington to plead for continued peace with the Plains Indians. His aide, Second Lieutenant Jim Gary, has been assigned to persuade General William T. Sherman that his plan for a military attack on the Comanche would be a deadly error. Meanwhile, Quanah Parker is organizing the Kiowa and Cheyenne to join him in an effort to drive the white buffalo hunters from the plains. As each side forms battle plans, a spark is all that is needed to ignite the frontier into total war!

NIGHTS OF TERROR
STEVE FRAZEE

The heart of the American West can be found in the Western fiction of Steve Frazee. This collection of eight short stories showcases Frazee's ability to produce suspense and excitement while capturing the past with impeccable historical accuracy and a deep understanding of human nature—including its dark side. In the title story, Frazee blends elements of a gripping thriller within a Western setting. Because of rustling, ranchers have taken to posting a guard at Big Ghost Basin. When three of those guards are killed, all the evidence points to a gigantic beast whose tracks match those of no known animal—a beast who's never been seen by anyone still alive!

WINTER KILL
COTTON SMITH

Rustling is an ugly business. Just the suspicion of it can get somebody hurt—or killed. And there's a whole lot of suspicion over on the Bar 6, the largest spread in the region. Old Titus Branson is missing a hundred head of Bar 6 cattle, and he's mighty sure of who did it: Bass Manko. Titus isn't about to sit still for something like that. He and his boys are dead set on seeing Manko swing from a rope. But Titus will have to face someone besides Manko first: Manko's best friend—Titus's own son!

TOM PICCIRILLI

Coffin Blues

Priest McClaren wants to put his past behind him. It's a past filled with loss, murder...and revenge. Now all Priest wants is to own a carpentry shop and earn a quiet living building coffins. But it looks like peace and quiet just aren't in Priest's future. His ex-lover has pleaded with him to carry ransom money into hostile territory in Mexico, to rescue her new husband. It's a mission he can't refuse, but it could also easily get him killed. Especially when he runs afoul of Don Braulio, a bandit with a great fondness for knives....